FREE TO WISH

AN AMARYLLIS SERIES NOVELLA

TRACEY JERALD

FREE TO WISH

Tracey Jerald

101 Marketside Avenue, Suite 404-205

Ponte Vedra, FL, 3208

https://www.traceyjerald.com

Book Layout © 2017 BookDesignTemplates.com

Free to Wish/ Tracey Jerald

ISBN: 978-1-7358129-1-5(eBook)

ISBN: 978-1-7358129-2-2 (Paperback)

Library of Congress Control Number: TBD

Editor: One Love Editing (http://oneloveediting.com/)

Proof Edits: Comma Sutra Editorial (https://www.facebook.com/CommaSutraEditorial)

Cover Design: Amy Queau – QDesign (https://www.qcoverdesign.com)

❀ Created with Vellum

To the friendships I made by taking a chance and kissing a frog. Because of you, the experience was as wonderful as finding a true storybook prince.

ALSO BY TRACEY JERALD

Amaryllis Series

Free - An amaryllis Prequel *(Newsletter Subscribers only)*

Free to Dream

Free to Run

Free to Rejoice

Free to Breathe

Free to Believe

Free to Live

Free to Dance

Free to Wish

Midas Series

Perfect Proposal

Perfect Assumption

Perfect Composition

Perfect Order (Fall 2021)

Standalones

Close Match

Ripple Effect

Unconditionally With Me – *A With Me in Seattle Novella*

Go to https://www.traceyjerald.com/ for all buy links!

PLAYLIST

Thomas Rhett, Maren Morris: "Craving You"
Marie Miller: "6'2"
Justin Bieber: "Sorry"
Stephen Puth: "Sexual Vibe"
Delta Rae: "Holding on to Good"
Shawn Mendes: "Mercy"
The Corrs, Bono: "When the Stars Go Blue"
Loreena McKennit: "The Mummer's Dance"
Avril Lavigne: "Head Above Water"
The Script, will.i.am: "Hall of Fame"
The Chainsmokers, Coldplay: "Something Just Like This"

THE LEGEND OF AMARYLLIS

There are variations regarding the legend of how amaryllis flowers came to be. Generally, the tale is told like this:

Amaryllis, a shy nymph, fell deeply in love with Alteo, a shepherd with great strength and beauty, but her love was not returned. He was too obsessed with his gardens to pay much attention to her.

Amaryllis hoped to win Alteo over by giving him the one thing he wanted most, a flower so unique it had never existed in the world before. She sought advice from the oracle Delphi and carefully followed his instructions. She dressed in white, and for thirty nights, appeared on Alteo's doorstep, piercing her heart with a golden arrow.

When Alteo finally opened his eyes to what was before him, he saw only a striking crimson flower that sprung from the blood of Amaryllis's heart.

It's not surprising the amaryllis has come to be the symbol of pride, determination, and radiant beauty. What's also not surprising is somehow, someway, we all bleed a little bit while we're falling in love.

PROLOGUE
FINN- PRESENT DAY

We're lying in our bed in our home in Connecticut with our newborn daughter snuggled in between us when Jenna tips her head, causing her long blonde hair to slip helplessly from the knot she's had it twisted in all day. I'd think it was one of the many dreams I'd had about her over the years, but this time, she raises tired eyes up to mine and murmurs, "Finally, it's just us."

I reach over, and my fingers feel the silkiness of her hair. I don't know who blessed me, but I offer up yet another thank-you before speaking. "I love our families, but heaven help me if another one of them knocks at the door—I may boot the lot of them to Ireland, including yours."

Jenna giggles softly before reaching to clasp my hand. "They can't help it, Finn. She's our first child, Mom and Dad and Em's first grand-daughter. And she's so..."

My "Perfect" comes out choked. Leaning forward, I touch my lips lightly to Jenna's before whispering, "Thank you."

"Surely not for cursing you so loudly the families could hear it in the waiting area."

"No, not for that. Nor for almost breaking my fingers, though I can appreciate why." I lean over and press my lips to our newborn daughter's head. "She has quite the noggin on her."

"Apparently our Hannah is going to be as smart as her daddy," Jenna boasts proudly.

I lift our joined hands to my lips before I correct her. "I think she's already showing signs of being more like her mother, Jenna. Just look at the evidence. First of all, she's exquisite."

Even after all this time, Jenna still blushes when I point out her obvious beauty. "Finn."

"And she's quite obviously the smartest baby in the world. She's mastered eating and clearly knows how to tell us all about when she's hungry or needs a new nappy."

Jenna bursts out laughing. "I think that's nature helping her along there, my love."

"And there's my irrefutable proof. Just like her mother, she captured my heart the moment I saw her. It was instantaneous." Jenna's dark eyes begin to well with tears. I release her hand only so I can brush them away. "Every minute that passes, I know I'm blessed you gave me the second chance I likely didn't deserve. I threw away love out of fear. I don't want Hannah to make our same mistakes."

"She won't. And if she does, we'll be there to guide her and support her." Jenna grabs my hand away from her face and holds it over our child like a benediction.

"No one will be good enough for her," I vow. And then I bark out a laugh. "God, now I sound like your father."

"Please, let's avoid that at all costs," she says wryly. And we both laugh with the memory of the first time I met her father not that long ago.

Just then, Jenna's stomach rumbles, and I push up on an elbow. "Are you finally hungry?"

She nods. "What do we have in the kitchen?"

"I don't..." And then I remember what we do have. The hidden blue box from Tiffany's with the diamond key I purchased with the peridot in the center. "I'll make you something." Rolling to the side of the bed, I wait until Jenna gets comfortable with Hannah in her arms before leaning over to kiss them both. "I'll be back."

"We'll be waiting. Won't we, Hannah? In the meanwhile, I have plenty of stories to tell you."

I'm smiling as I leave our room, but then I come up short. Ducking my head back in, I interrupt Jenna telling Hannah about the antics of her "Crazy Uncle Phil."

"Jenna?"

"Yes?"

We have years. She won't need the knowledge for a long time, but something inside me pushes me to ask, "You won't tell her about us without me there. Will you?"

A tender smile crosses Jenna's face. "Go get me some food. And I'll wait until you come back before I tell your daughter how—despite you bungling our start—we managed to fall in love."

Relief floods through me. I whistle an old Irish lullaby I remember my grandfather humming for my sister, Maura, before I raid the refrigerator to make a Tayto sandwich or two since my family just replenished our supplies before I threw everyone out to have some time with just my girls.

And memories that are never too far from my heart.

2

JENNA

Five years earlier

Three of us fall into the bar in a tumble of cloaks and blonde hair, much to the vaguely amused looks of the few Parisians who even bothered to glance in our direction. Shoving mine fully off my head, I declare, "It's exactly how Lynne described it to me," naming my best friend, who unfortunately couldn't take time off work to meet us in Paris for Fashion Week.

The second—and tallest—slips off her chic hood that's been doing a dual purpose of hiding her face from the ever-present paparazzi and keeping the fine mist away from her flat-ironed hair. "It's something all right. Are you certain we're not going to die of food poisoning in here?" My cousin Danielle's brows arch over her infamous violet eyes as she takes in the questionable scents emanating from the kitchen.

The third in our trio shakes out her golden curls, sending them bouncing in every direction. Behind her trademark red glasses, my stepmother Emily Freeman's blue eyes dance with mirth. "Jenna, this is fabulous. It reminds me of Tide Pool back in Collyer, just with food."

"Which is exactly what Lynne said to me months ago when she

found this place while on a business trip for Ryan." I motion toward a free table to the bartender, who simply waves his hand in the universal manner most have, letting me know it's free. Once we sit, I inform them both proudly, "She's been to Paris at least ten times since she started working for Lockwood Industries."

"I'm so proud of her—of both of you." Em leans over and kisses my cheek.

"Me too, Little Miss. Now, if we could figure out what's safe to consume," Dani bemoans.

I roll my eyes. "You know, you keep it up, I can always arrange for us to go back. I mean, did you both want to answer more questions from reporters after the show?"

They both groan in unison before answering, "No."

"But what was wrong with one of our hotel rooms?" Dani demands.

Every time I'm in one, it reminds me how lonely I am. The words almost escape before I manage to lasso them in. Instead, I flash my cousin a beady-eyed glare. "What happened to your sense of adventure?"

"I lost it after standing for the fourth hour in five-inch heels," she returns.

Em, always the peacemaker, pats Dani's arm. "And this is why we have a day at the spa booked for tomorrow."

Feeling a little guilty, I relent. "We'll just have one drink if you're that tired. It's just so great to have you both here, and I rarely get to explore when I'm out of town for business."

Dani reaches across the table and twines her fingers with mine. "Darling, I'm just being a diva. You know there isn't anyone I'd rather be with than you."

My lips curve with pure feminine understanding and a healthy dose of appreciation. "Liar. You're just upset Brendan isn't here to reap the rewards of tonight being such a success."

My cousin, not just any model but the face that covers magazines all over the world and who is dating the world's most famous country music star, tosses back her gorgeous head and hoots out a laugh.

"You're absolutely right. Why did he have to go to that silly premiere?"

"Gee, Dani? Because he wrote the score? It's the same reason Jake isn't here for me and his oldest daughter." Em bestows a brilliant smile on our waiter, who I place at being all of seventeen. And judging by the way his eyes dart between the three of us, he isn't sure which of us he's suddenly madly in love with.

"Une bouteille de votre meilleur champagne, s'il vous plaît?" I engage his attention. And feel a sweet tug in a region of my chest I would have sworn was dead except for members of my family and my closest of friends when his jaw falls open.

He nods and sighs but doesn't move an inch until a rapidly shouted order from the bar grabs his attention and he scurries off.

"Look at you, Miss Thing." Dani's voice holds a note of admiration.

"What?"

"It wasn't that long ago your father was bemoaning his worries about your future and wondering if you were going to live a life of crime, and yet here you are, international marketing wonder and ordering in fluent French."

My face flames at the reminder of my not-too-distant past. "I picked it up from Lynne."

"What? The attitude or..."

"The French," I grit out as our waiter hurriedly arrives back at our table with a familiar label and three glasses. "It's kind of like knowing how to ask for tequila and beer in Mexico on spring break. And before you both can ask, yes, we did that there during college as well."

"Good," Em says simply. I'm not surprised though. Ever since I met her when I was sixteen, she's been my inspiration, my champion, even within a family of them that I was absorbed into when my father married her. "You work hard and deserve to have fun, Jenna. Just as long as it's safe and makes you happy."

For just a moment, the overhead light catches on the silver rim of the glass, reminding me of the glint in *his* eyes the first time I'd challenged him on some overblown theory he was trying to teach. And every time after until that final time when he blew my heart clean out of my chest.

The door whips open, and for just a moment, my heart thuds against my ribs as a tall, broad-shouldered man steps into the tavern. But I swiftly mask my disappointment once I realize it isn't him—it never is—by beaming at our young waiter, who offers me a sip of the uncorked Dom Perignon. "*Merci.*" I hand him back the glass, which he quickly refills, along with Dani's and Em's.

"And another heart falls splat at Jenna's feet." Dani's laughter peals out once we're again alone.

"Don't be ridiculous. I'm not careless with something like that," I snap back, perhaps a bit harsher than I intend.

Em's hand slides over mine and offers a comforting squeeze. "Of course not."

Slightly mollified, I take a long drink of champagne before nodding to acknowledge her words.

She scoots closer. "You know, you have a family that loves you, Jenna. Regardless of whatever you need."

I roll the excellent champagne on my tongue, despite the fact it's suddenly lingering bitterly. "What makes you think I need anything?" I counter.

Em and Dani exchange complicated glances. I demand, "No, tell me. You think I'm unhappy with my life?"

"I think there's something troubling you," Em corrects gently. "It's been festering for some time."

I lift my glass again to my lips, praying neither woman will notice the tremble in my hand that betrays my darkest thoughts, my greatest pain, and yet, my secret wish. "I'm fine."

"No woman has ever used those words strung together to describe her emotions and not wanted to chop off the balls from some man," Dani declares outrageously.

I place my flute down before breaking into peals of laughter. "Thank goodness Uncle Phil isn't here—Em would have spit in his face."

Em leans in. "I'll let you both in on a little secret."

Dani and I eagerly lean closer.

"Half the time I do, it's completely intentional. My darling brother is a complete pain in the ass."

And that sets the three of us off into screaming laughter. Dabbing at the tears welling in my eyes, I admit, "I needed to laugh tonight. I needed both of you. I just wanted to forget for a while."

"What did you need to forget?" Em slips in quickly.

And so, I confide in them what up until this point only Lynne knew. After all, when you burst into your apartment with your heart shattered into a million pieces, there's only one way to put it back together—with unconditional love.

Em scoots closer. "Jenna, honey, why didn't you say anything before now about this Professor O'Roarke?"

God, I just love the way she sneers his name. It warms up something that's been growing colder inside of me as time's passed. "I thought I could outrun the feelings."

"Other men?" Dani probes gently.

I shrug. "Not many. With Finn—that's his given name—I felt like my body, my heart touched the stars. With other men, well, I felt like I had to."

"Had to?" Em questions.

"Not in that sense," I quickly assure her. "I forced myself to take that step towards intimacy to prove to myself I could. That maybe enough time had passed that my heart had healed from what happened."

"And how did you feel afterwards?" Dani lays her hand over mine.

"Dissatisfaction and disappointment, much like I felt about sex in college before I walked into my international marketing class the first time and saw *him*. In other words, nothing's changed." I lift my glass and glug some of the fine alcohol. As I right my head, my hair slides into my face. Unconsciously, I shrug my shoulders to move my hair back. "I think coming home for a while, being with the family, will be good for me."

Em snorts. "It will certainly keep your mind off of things. Ali has something lined up for you that makes a cake of Corinna's look like a paltry welcome-home gift."

My heart knocks against my ribs, but I still maintain my composure. "Really? Such as?"

"I was going to save this as a surprise, but Amaryllis Events is getting a full-page spread in *Promoter Quarterly*. They're sending out both an interviewer and a photographer. And they want an exclusive with you." Em points at me. I'm certain my jaw is unhinged as Em continues. "In fact, the article was being pitched as *Amaryllis Events - A Legendary Force. With Jenna Madison Leading the Marketing Helm, They're Changing Weddings Around the Globe.*"

Finally, I manage to speak. "That's crazy. It's the six of you. Cass and Ali. Corrina with the cakes, Phil with the flowers. You're the genius behind the designs. And Holly's photos. If it wasn't for any of you..."

But Em interrupts me. "And if the word doesn't get out, no one would know about us. God, Jenna, Ali may kiss you in front of the entire family."

"Why? Are the numbers that good?"

"They're better than she could ever have predicted. And this magazine? They're giving up the cover, the lead article, and while all of us will be in it—Dani, they want you too—" Dani lifts her glass in acknowledgment. "—it's all about how a twenty-three-year-old tapped into the gold mine of the social media movement."

I can't form words. Even if I could, I'm certain the first ones would be a grand ole fuck-you to the professor who tried to mold my mind long before he screwed my body. "We did it. We're a team," I manage to choke out.

"No, sweetheart. You did. You believed in our dreams. You breathed new life into them and ran with them. Now, it's your turn to make a wish because you're as much a part of Amaryllis Events, Amaryllis Designs, as we are."

Even as the first tear spills over, I say huskily, "You literally saved me, Em. You're the reason I'm sitting here."

And just like that, her own eyes mist. The only noise is the clanking of drinks around the small bar. Finally, Em clears her throat. "I'll always be here if you need me, Jenna. Just because you're a grown woman doesn't mean you can't lean on your family. It just means we're still here for when big things happen, and you really do need us. But it's your time to shine, darling."

Dani lifts her glass. "I'd like to propose a toast."

Dutifully, Em and I lift our glasses. Dani leans in. "To you, Jenna. For growing up from a potential juvenile delinquent—" We all laugh before Dani continues. "—to a woman of substance. You're a woman with a sharp mind and an enormous capacity for love."

"Hear, hear." Em tips her glass against Dani's before the ping rings against mine.

I want to contradict them, but something holds me back. And I realize it's the truth. I do have an enormous capacity for love.

And if Professor Finn O'Roarke didn't want it, someone someday will.

About a month later, my skin is burning up under the photographer's lamps as shot after shot is being taken. Wearing a formfitting sleek black dress Em designed and a pair of Christian Louboutin heels that makes my legs appear a million miles long, I cross them easily. Briefly, I remember a time when such a simple gesture would have been a Herculean feat.

Has it been only seven years since Em saved my life from the drunk driver that almost took it? I wonder as I prop my chin on my fist and stare directly into the camera's unyielding lens. Someone shifts behind the equipment, and I can just make out my father's broad shoulders as he roams proudly in the back. So much changed that night—my relationship with him, the path I was put on to forgive my mother for being absent for much of my life, and the pathway to my future with the Freemans. All of them.

While it was Em who literally used the air from her own lungs to keep me alive in the precious moments before the transport to the hospital made it to us, it was her family who made room for us in their hearts. Despite the long shot of them making it themselves with the backgrounds they came from.

"Hold that look, Jenna," the photographer orders.

"Do you mind sharing what you're thinking about?" the reporter inquires from the side.

"Family pride. I'm remembering the story about how Amaryllis Events started and the amount of sacrifice, love, and dedication necessary for the family to do so." And the pain. "Each family member endured those emotions individually and together to bring us to this very moment."

"Not unlike the legend of the Amaryllis," the reporter returns.

"No, not so very different. But I've learned if you're passionate about something, you'll bleed for it."

"Can I quote you on that?"

That's when I feel a hand land on my shoulder. It squeezes gently. My eyes drift to the side to meet the aqua-colored ones of Cassidy, Em's slightly older sister. Her eyes drift over my head. Twisting in my seat, I jolt when I realize they're all standing behind me, supporting me, just like they have since they brought me into their family as one of their own: Phil, Corinna, Ali, Holly, and, of course, my Em.

My savior.

My chin lifts slightly as the honor they instilled in me about family, life, and love tumbles clean through me. No matter what happened in the past, I will no longer live with regrets. I loved. And I will love again. But I learned from the wall of strength behind me a heart can be shattered, and with the right repairs, it can beat on.

So, there's a fierce pride in my voice when I simply respond, "Yes."

Right before I'm again blinded by the light of the camera flash.

What feels like ages later, we're informed the article will run in their late-May edition. Ali's smile is sphinxlike as she thanks the reporter and crew. As for me, my mind is already whirling as I begin planning the long-term social media impact. The minute the conference room at the mansion is cleared, I turn toward Em and say,

"Expect orders for the spring line to increase by twenty percent. Fall is going to go crazy the minute I can leak something, anything, about the materials you're using—a silhouette, anything."

"Before we do anything else, we just have one thing to do first." Cassidy walks up with a small jewelry box.

I turn the box over and over in my hand. "What's this?"

Em has moved into Dad's arms. Phil has his arms around Corinna and Holly. Ali has moved next to Cassidy before urging, "Open it, Jenna."

I do, and my hand flies immediately to my mouth. "Oh, my God." It's a pair of earrings cast in gold. Each one is a perfect amaryllis with an arrow piercing them. My eyes fill with unshed tears.

Ali muses, "We thought to save them until Christmas, but we decided this was more personal."

"I don't need these." A hush races around the room. A single tear escapes. "I just need all of you."

Somehow, I'm unsurprised it's Em who is the first to reach me. And in my ear she whispers, "You are loved, Jenna Madison. This is our way of reminding you of that."

Before I can respond, I'm pulled from Em and passed around the sisters and Phil. Then I carefully remove the pearls I wore for the interview and slip in tangible proof that love built on anything but respect, trust, and faith isn't love at all.

It's nothing but a foolish wish.

3

FINN

Six months later

I wish for so much, things that are so long past I'll never be able to fix them. There are some things that should be left in the past, even if it leaves my heart aching. Especially on a night like tonight.

No, I'll never be deserving of inhaling her sweet scent, more potent than the wildflowers that cluster along the coast during the summer not too far from where I'm standing. But that's not what's important. Her happiness is.

I just was foolish enough to have thrown away my right to be a part of it.

Staring up at the first star as it appears over my family's farm, a familiar longing washes over me. *Jenna.* She's never far from my mind, my heart. From the first moment I tasted her, I handed her a part of my soul.

And I'll never wish her gone despite how painful it is to know there's little to no chance I'll ever see her again.

Wincing, I still recall every single word she hurled at me after I refused to admit to her, to myself, there was more between us than a mere lapse of my self-control. She was my student; I thirteen years her senior. The lines I crossed were many. But still, I thought to seek her out to explain, to soften the distraught look she flung at me as she ran from my classroom that glorious May afternoon.

When I finally gave in to the urge and hauled her against me. When I kissed her. When...

I planned on righting things between us until I received the phone call about my grandfather's passing mere moments later—a phone call that changed everything. It's been three and a half years, and I'm still only vaguely aware of jumping on the first transatlantic flight carrying me home. I'm still not certain how I even booked the damned thing.

The next few days saw a few terse emails sent to the administrative staff at UConn to pack up my things to have them shipped, pleaded with another professor to grade my final exams, and survived the loss of a man who was the heart and soul of our clan.

After the initial grief passed, I began to make plans to return to my job in Connecticut. I had hopes of tracking down Jenna, having heard through student talk that she was a Connecticut native. That is until I realized the financial mess my family's legacy was in. Once I realized there was a very real chance my grandmother would be uprooted from the farm she'd lived on with my grandfather for close to sixty years, I knew there was no returning to America to chase after a beautiful young woman.

That left me wondering what in bleeding hell happened to all the euros my grandfather had borrowed? I found out from my grandmother the fecked-up lot of my relatives—including my own parents, who'd borrowed money to go on their last dig in Africa but couldn't quite manage to haul their asses home for my grandfather's funeral—had no qualms about holding out a hand. Now, as the oldest of the next generation, the mess fell to me. My cousins, so proud of the financial success I'd achieved on my own, looked to me to solve the problem.

So compounded with my despair for losing a man I loved and respected, I spent months obtaining the legal right to pay off the note with the bank so my grandmother could live out her days where she spent the ones she lived and loved. Leaving myself exactly where I'd worked so hard to leave—back on the farm in Clare, figuring out what I could do to support my family and still be the man I need to be.

Three years later and I have no more answers other than the wink of gratitude in my grandmother's eyes when I help her climb to the spot where my grandfather proposed—where I'm currently standing.

Several times in the early months, I debated trying to email Jenna on her school addy, but what was I to say? That I was a scut, a useless sod? Yes, blast it, I was. I even drafted a few. But nothing sounded right. Either they were too austere or insignificant rubbish. No, I should have spoken with her before I left, I conclude grimly. And now? There is nothing I can do, nothing to offer her. What would I do but trap her here? Give up the bright lights and big cities she's visiting for a seaside farm here in Burren?

Jenna has a bright future ahead of her while mine is filled with family as I used my last dime to salvage my grandfather's last wish— that generations of O'Roarkes would tread the land beneath my feet. I'm recovering, using a portion of the money the farm my grandmother settled upon me to build a very healthy nest egg for myself.

But I'm a long way from the woman who carelessly wore nine-hundred-dollar shoes in a photo shoot.

My jaw clenches. *I did what you asked, seanáthair.* Now, as the new star blinks at me, I make a wish. *I hope your life will be filled with nothing but happiness, my beautiful Jenna.*

I finally admitted to myself I fell head over heels for Jenna during that last semester teaching at UConn. Looking back, I figure it was somewhere between arguing whether Dale Carnegie would have been as effective in the age of social media and realizing the silk skirt that encased her arse needed to be in a puddle on the floor around my bed.

"But you killed whatever could have been between you both. You made her believe your coming together was nothing more than an interlude, just sex." I can hear the profound disgust in my own voice. The reality is it was something so much more. I just didn't realize it until I wished for her by my side mere minutes after she slammed out of my classroom.

Shoving my hands deep in the pockets of my trousers, I tip my head back and wonder what she would do if I tried to reach out to her now that I know where she is. After all, that's what drove me out into the dusk. Jenna's done more than just fly; she's soared. I always knew she would. Tonight, my heart almost stopped when I flipped the page of *Promoter Quarterly*, an internationally renowned economics magazine, to find a multiple-page spread on her prolific use of social media to promote the one-of-a-kind business for Amaryllis Events, growing the business 500 percent in one year.

After I recovered from seeing her gorgeous face challenging me from the glossy two-dimensional pages, I felt both a surge of pride and equal despair. After all, why would fearless Jenna ever want to risk her heart again with someone who was afraid to give it to her the first time?

A cane on the flagstone alerts me to another's presence. I call out, "I thought we agreed a while ago about you walking all this way on your own, *seanmháthair*?"

"Your *deirfiúr* helped me." Of course, my baby sister, Maura, wouldn't let our grandmother walk the distance from the house to the path. I almost manage a smile as my grandmother steps up next to me. "You're thinking about her again?"

"When am I not?" Quickly, I fill in my grandmother about seeing her in the article.

"Then do something about it!" she snaps. "You wish and you think, but you spend too much time doing just that. Act on it, Finn. Thinking about things won't give you the answers you need to move on."

I resume my brooding. "She will find love, *seanmháthair*. With a good man."

"And you do not think that is you, my Finn?" She reaches my side and hooks her hand inside the crook of my arm. "Why is that?"

I wince. "If you knew the dishonorable way I behaved toward her, *seanmháthair*, you would find the strength to paddle me."

Her snowy-white brow raises in challenge. "You think I could not manage it anyway?"

I bark out a short laugh. "I have little doubt you could manage it." But I resume my silence in hopes she will let it drop.

"Finn, what are you doing in this place?"

I'm shocked by the question. "Excuse me?"

She leans into me. "This isn't what you dreamed of. You are Professor Finn O'Roarke. You worked hard to become that man. Go be that man." She lifts her cane and points in the direction of the sea, unerringly pointing it in the direction that would carry me across the ocean toward Jenna.

"It's not that simple."

"Then explain it to me." She breaks away and moves to sit on a natural stone bench.

I kneel at her feet before taking her hand in mine. Slowly, I weigh my words in my mind. "I fought what I was feeling for her for a long time."

"Because she was your student," my grandmother confirms.

"Yes. She was of legal age." I pause as my grandmother frowns. "Jenna is thirteen years younger than I am, *seanmháthair*. She was twenty when..."

"When your souls met," she concludes.

I lay my head on her knee, something I've done since I was a little boy. "Yes. But I...I made her feel like it was less...ow!" I yell as she slaps my ear. I mutter something completely foul.

"Don't you dare use that language with me, Finnegan! How dare you treat the woman of your heart like that?" she snaps.

"She didn't let me. She was unshakeable."

"Good for her."

"And just as I was about to go after her, I received the call about *seanáthair*."

She says something rude, which has my eyebrows winging upward. "Do I get to wash your mouth out with soap for that kind of language, young lady?" I make a tsking sound.

She flushes but makes no apologies for her gutter mouth. "Your grandfather's timing was notoriously awful."

I blink for just a moment before I toss my head back and roar with laughter. "Oh, that's rich. What makes you say such a wicked thing?"

"Well, he'd often begin to...just as you children...never mind. We're talking about your Jenna."

The grin on my face at the idea of all of us interrupting my grandparents' romantic antics dies. "She's not my Jenna. I gave up that right."

"Then change it." She pushes to her feet, almost dumping me to my back. "You're going to have your chance."

I scramble to my feet. "What do you mean?"

"Maura came over tonight to talk to both of us. Will finally proposed." She holds out her arm.

I take it and begin to guide her down the stone steps, grumbling, "It's about time. They've been together for years."

"She's talking about an enormous wedding already," Grandmother says serenely.

"Of course she is," I groan, knowing I'm not going to deny my baby sister a single thing. I come to an abrupt halt. "She's going to want the sun, the moon, and the stars for a wedding."

My grandmother leans up and pats my cheek. "I was thinking more about the dress. Wouldn't it be lovely if she had a special dress she could pass along to the next generation? Something like I saw in that magazine you left on the counter, perhaps?"

"*Seanmháthair*, I imagine it will take years to get her a dress like that," I caution her.

"Well, they weren't in any hurry to get engaged, now were they?" Before I can protest at this loving woman's attempt to help right the wrongs she finds in my life, she cautions me, "Finn, you might see this woman again and may not feel what you did. But regardless of what happens, I want you to have the chance. Love requires you to be tenacious. And if your Jenna is more than the one who got away, leave no stone unturned." Her head whips around, and her eyes water. "Your grandfather didn't."

I give her a moment before I lead her down the stairs, where I find Maura waiting to show me the beautiful diamond on the third finger of her left hand. But before I walk with them down the worn path back to the farm, I take a final glance over my shoulder at the star shining high in the early evening sky. And I make a wish.

Give me a chance to show you my heart, Jenna. I'll swear you'll never regret it.

4

JENNA

"I don't want to make any more wishes," I say fiercely to the warm Dublin night. "They hurt too much."

No sooner do the words come out of my mouth than I feel selfish for saying them. I'm living the kind of fantasy women daydream about. The glamour of being the worldwide spokeswoman for Amaryllis Events was exactly the sort of excitement I craved the first few years once I graduated college. I've traveled all over the world, witnessing brides falling in love with my stepmother's designs. But I'm so exhausted of pretending my own heartache hasn't abated each time I help a bride select her perfect gown from one of Emily's stunning dresses.

Taking a sip of cuvée blanche, I roll the candied apricot and orange flavors over my tongue as I think about how I came to be standing here.

I was practically born into the world of fashion, but it wasn't until Em came into our lives and showed me how much she pours into each of her designs that I realized fashion is a lot like falling in love. You have to be willing to bleed, to drown, to die. And as I've learned, rubbing a hand over my still-aching heart, I've done that once. And once was more than enough.

"Admit it, Jenna. You want the fairy tale. It simply just doesn't exist," I mock myself lightly as I stand in the open window letting the night air in.

Then again, he ran first—my fingers clench the iron balustrade—right after he took me in his classroom after I turned in my marketing final when I was twenty. My last class. He ripped the paper out of my hand, tossed it down, and...

Hearing a familiar blip, I'm torn from the memories as I quickly make my way across the room. I answer the FaceTime call and sigh a little inside when mahogany-brown eyes light up as he sees my face. "Why don't I hear yelling? Shouldn't the kids be home with you?" I tease my father gently.

"Shouldn't you be in bed?"

Propping my chin on my hand, I arch a brow. "Really, Dad? It's early here. Maybe I was debating going out in a few hours." I exaggerate the truth a bit. The only thing I'm debating at the ripe old age of twenty-five is the comfort of my bed. Alone.

"I don't want to know. These are the kinds of things you share with Em."

I flutter my lashes at him. "Listen, the stories I hear about you..."

"Are lies. Filthy lies, Jenna."

I laugh. "You always seem to know when to call."

"Feeling a bit blue, baby? Anything you want to talk to your old man about?"

"Just preparing for the next few days. You know how crazy things get once we start the final fittings."

My father groans. "Don't I ever. I've heard Em talk about this kind of white-glove service for years. Speaking of which, she's shoving me out of the way."

His face is replaced by that of my stepmother. I smile as the woman whose name has been heralded in bridal fashion along with Hailey Paige, Reem Acra, and Rivini in recent years beams at me. "Hey, Em."

"God, Jenna. You're stunning. I still remember you at sixteen. Seeing you makes me proud and old."

I laugh. "Stick with proud, Em. You're not that much older than I am." And another arrow of pain pierces my heart. Em's just a few years older than he is. Quickly shoving the thought aside, I ask, "Is there anything I need to know about tomorrow?"

Em launches into a litany of last-minute items I take careful note of. "Maura is a dream of a bride, Jenna. Her whole family will be with her for the fitting. They're very close."

I smirk. "I already reserved the largest room there is, Em. How many am I talking? Six, eight?"

"Fourteen."

I choke on a laugh. "Fourteen?"

"Generations of love in a single room. One day, I hope that's what we're building to leave to our children," she says whimsically.

Setting aside work, I tell her, "You are—you have. Years from now, Freeman family members will be gathering in much the same way."

"Well, we're counting on all of you to do that for us."

I shake my head. "I'm a Madison, not a Freeman," I remind her.

"You're family, Jenna," Em scolds me.

And in that moment, the words just rush out. "You've been everything to me, Em. You're my inspiration for so much."

"Damn you, Jenna. How long until you're coming home? I need to hug you."

"Ten days," I remind her.

"Not soon enough," she grumbles.

My heart, so anxious before, settles. I'm heading back to exactly what I left—a bedrock of love built on respect, trust, and faith. "I better let you go. Tomorrow's a long day," I tell her.

"I know. And Jenna?"

"Hmm?"

"Sometimes it's better to talk to someone about what's really wrong. Holding it all in doesn't help."

"Asking me something, Em?" I challenge her.

"No, just speaking from experience. We love you."

"I know. Love all of you." I press End to finish the call.

I don't know why I woke up with a

 feeling of apprehension coursing through my veins. I feel like cursing the ridiculously blue sky, considering my past chased me into my dreams, but somehow I find that impossible. Passing St. Stephen's Green, my heels make a staccato sound on the stone streets as I turn down Grafton, where the exclusive bridal salon that wisely chose to stock Amaryllis Designs is located.

A chill races down the back of my neck as the feeling I'm being watched almost causes me to trip over a slightly upturned paver. "That's ridiculous," I snap. "You hardly know anyone here." But even as I say the words aloud, I know I should be cautious. I can only imagine what the male members of my family would say if I ignored my instincts. "Keene would blow a gasket," I mutter just as my fingers touch the handle to the discreet glass door that hides the bridal salon above.

When I hear, "Who's Keene, Jenna?" I freeze. There's no way Finn O'Roarke just asked me that question. Ignoring my hallucination, I swing open the door and step forward to press the button for the small lift. Miraculously the doors open, and I move inside and press the button for the second floor before my head falls forward in agony.

Maybe it's being here in this city. All these sights and sounds that remind me of him, I think desperately.

Then I hear footsteps, slow and measured, bringing someone onto the elevator before the doors swoosh shut.

"I can't find the words for how lovely you are." When he speaks again, I realize fate's just a cruel bitch making me see him again.

"There's no way you said that to me," I hiss.

"Why not?" Finn's scent overwhelms me in a devastating way. It feels like yesterday instead of five damn years since I've been this close to him. I feel his hand smooth over my shoulder, dragging his fingers over the bronze silk of my dress.

My eyes pop open, and I see his gray eyes fixed on my lips. He leans down, his intent obvious when the elevator dings behind him.

My hand slams up against his chest. Shoving him aside, I manage to slip through the doors before they close. I jeer, "Because you told me I was nothing but a little girl who needed to wish upon a few stars to find her prince."

He winces. "Jenna..."

"Save it, Finn. Or should I still be calling you Professor O'Roarke?" I mock as I back out of the elevator.

"You didn't ask what I was doing here!" he yells after me.

I still before I turn and inform him coolly, "I have too much to do to care." With that parting shot, I pivot and make my way down the hall.

I have to make it through today before I can process the fact I know Finn is in Dublin. I have to finish the job I was sent here to do.

Then I can do what I did last time.

Cry.

5

FINN

J enna Madison was a temptation at twenty when she sat in my international marketing class. There was a preposterous pull between us from the second she walked in the door. There was no way I'd have predicted that behind fathomless brown eyes was a woman whose brain was light-years ahead of my own. Jenna openly challenged me on some of the theories I was teaching, not only substantiating her arguments with fact but with practical experience.

Fuck, I'm surprised I didn't make a move on her before she turned in that last exam. But after I touched her, after I tasted her, after I sank my cock inside of her, I turned on her from the guilt I felt afterward. Jenna didn't deserve it. And to be honest, I'm not sure I've slept a full night since.

I was a real prince because I didn't just break her heart that day—I broke my own.

"No one's ever made me feel like this, Finn," she breathed just as I wrenched my lips from hers, my cock still throbbing. "I swear no one ever will."

I hesitated. "Jenna, you're a beautiful girl, but..."

"But what?" Her hand trembled.

Despite my insides churning, I did what I knew to be best. I pulled away even as I lifted a hand to smooth her silky hair that was mussed due to my hands fisting it. "But someday, you're going to wish upon the right star to find your prince. He's just not me."

Wrenching back, Jenna whispered, "You can't be serious."

"I am. I'm..."

"Don't you dare say you're sorry."

I didn't. Instead, I held it in while I watched a single tear trail down her face. Just one before she backed away, righting her clothes.

When she reached the door, she clutched the jamb. "Thank you for reminding me of what I'm really looking for."

And being the stupid feck I was, I asked, "What's that?"

"A love built on respect, trust, and faith." Then she swept out the door and out of my life.

That was the last image I had of her until I saw her face in *Promoters Quarterly*. That night I searched her name and found her in Rome. Berlin. Moscow. All over the bloody Americas. And each time I saw her face, I called myself a fool.

Making my way down the hall toward the bridal salon, I realize something critical has changed—the exuberance and passion that lit her from within are hidden.

"*An áit thíos atá ceapaithe duit, a dhiabhal.*" I wish myself to the depths of hell as I hear a door slam at the far end of the hallway.

My grandmother used to pray God would never grant us peace with the way we used to get underfoot as children. As I pressed the bell, I mutter, "Well, *seanmháthair*, are you happy?"

Interminable moments pass before the sound of the tumblers click. "What do you want?" Jenna demands.

Everything, but that's not what I say. "I believe we have an appointment."

And just like that long-ago afternoon, every ounce of blood drains from her beautiful face. Unlike then, there's no passionate outburst. All she does is murmur, "O'Roarke. Of course. Come right this way. The bride is due to arrive any moment."

I step inside and into a different world—Jenna's world.

And immediately, I'm fascinated as the student becomes the teacher.

Several hours later, my baby sister is glowing.

"Finn, I feel beautiful." Her face tips up with joy.

"*Mo sicín beag*, you've always been beautiful. This dress just makes you more so," I declare resolutely.

Even as her eyes fill, she punches me. "Don't call me your little chicken."

Lifting her hand to my heart, I remind her, "You always have been. Will is a lucky man."

Maura huffs. "I had to work hard enough to make him believe it."

"Sometimes, we're foolish," I murmur. Out of the corner of my eye, I notice Jenna stiffen before her professionalism kicks in.

"Maura, I hate to interrupt, but we need to get you out of that dress so the alterations team can make those small adjustments in time for your big day."

Although my sister is reluctant, Jenna coaxes her behind a velvet curtain again. While she does so, I escort my family to the main salon. My grandmother grips my arm. "She's the one."

I don't try to deny it. "Yes." After my abrupt departure from America mere hours after Jenna and I connected, weeks before she graduated, it was my family's farm where I remained to lick my self-inflicted wounds. One night, I told my grandmother about how I found my heart in America and let it go because she was so young.

And she called me a fool. "The heart is powered by many things, Finn. Age isn't one of them."

It wasn't long after I saw Jenna's face for the first time representing this American designer. I've been following her, waiting for the right moment to approach.

That moment is now.

"You owe her an apology," she scolds me.

"If she'll allow it" is all I'm able to get out before the object of my every desire joins us.

Jenna moves directly to my sister. "I hope the dress was everything you hoped for?"

"It was everything I wished for," Maura corrects.

I'm the only one who notices Jenna's slight flinch at the word. "All the better. I was asked to pass this along to you." Jenna crosses to her desk and slips an envelope from the leather bag she was carrying earlier. "Congratulations on your nuptials from all of us at Amaryllis Events," she pronounces.

Maura frowns. "What's this?"

Jenna smiles mysteriously, causing my cock to harden. "Open it and see."

We all gather closer as Maura opens the clasp and then gasps. "Is this...me?"

"It's like looking into a photograph," I declare.

And that's when the woman I fell for five bloody long years ago shines through.

"Emily will be thrilled. It's something she does only for her custom-made designs, much like the special markings on each of the dresses." Jenna's face glows with love when she talks about this woman.

Despite my overwhelming desire, there's a hole in my chest. I told her to wish, and now she has this whole other life. I have less than nine days to convince her to take a chance on one with me. After I give her a long-overdue apology.

I linger behind as everyone makes their way out. "That was a lovely touch."

"Hmm?" Jenna's collecting her bag and swinging it up on her shoulder.

"The drawing," I clarify.

"The people I work with are generous with their hearts."

It's the opening I've been waiting for. "And are you, Jenna?" At her quizzical look, I rephrase my question. "Are you generous—perhaps with your time? Maybe long enough for me to offer a proper apology?"

"What for, Professor? Not grading my final exam high enough? I still pulled out an A," she mocks as she storms through the salon doors. Instead of the elevator, she hurries down the stairs. We don't speak until we reach the street.

I frown as I reach for her arm. "Have you changed so much in five years, Jenna?"

"Why do you care? I found I learned a lot from you, Professor. Should I genuflect, or would a simple thank-you suffice?"

"It's Finn, Jenna. And I'm sure whatever success you've attained is well-earned. Perhaps can we take a moment to talk about what happened?"

"There's no need," she shoots back. "Let's keep it on the same level you left it. Over."

"Where I left it was wrong," I say gently.

"Really? Which part of it was so wrong?"

"The part where I..." I begin, but Jenna interrupts.

"All damn semester you kept giving me signs you were as hungry as I was for something more. I wasn't so naïve, nor was I so innocent, not to recognize them. So, Professor, you can take your apology and get the hell away from me. You told me to wish on a star—well, surprise. I did."

"What did you wish for?" My heart aches at the bitterness in her voice.

"I wished for a man who would take one look at me and recognize me for what I am—worthy." She seethes. "Since you determined that wasn't you, I'll be professional as I help your sister's dreams come true. Then we never have to see each other again."

God, the pain her words cause. "Don't you want an explanation?"

"What's the point?" She tosses her long hair. I want to sink my hands into it again before I lift her mouth up to mine. "Nine days. You only have to have to deal with me until the ceremony's over. Then I'll be gone."

My nostrils flare as her words burn through me. "What makes you think I want that?"

"Who says you have a choice? In fact—" She approaches me, hips swaying. "—I'm damn certain you never gave me one." Her fingertip drags down the front of my shirt.

I grab her hand. "Be careful, little girl," I growl.

"Why, Professor?" Her lips curve. "Your factual assumption still needs correction, I see."

"Oh?" I can barely get the word out when she presses the lean length of her body against mine.

She rises up on her tiptoes to whisper in my ear, "I wasn't a little girl then, and I'm sure as fuck not one now." She goes to pull away.

Too bad for her because my arm's around her waist, hauling her back to exactly where she was. My head's already lowering when I whisper, "Thank Christ for that."

Then I kiss her.

6

JENNA

Somehow, we manage to make it back to the Merrion without bursting into flames. Dragging me close, he murmurs, "You have about three seconds to decide where—your room or mine?" I'm confused until I remember the wedding is taking place here at the hotel.

"Mine." Because later, I want the scent of him wrapped around me when I cry. If my fairy tale only includes two moments of love to cherish, I want to linger over them as long as I can.

Once inside the elevator, Finn backs me against the wall near the buttons. Pressing one, he begins to feast on my neck. "How do you know what room I'm in?" I manage to gasp out.

"Because your room is right next door to mine, *mo chroí.*" My head jerks back at the proclamation, but before I can get any words out, Finn's lips are devouring mine.

He silences any questions with deep, hungry kisses as he frames my face with his large hands. How could I have forgotten how delicate he made me feel? I think wildly as I shove my hands beneath his jacket, eager to be touching him. His tongue and mine stroke against one another over and over until a ping notifies us of our arrival.

"Quickly now." Finn drags me behind him. Despite having

followed him through the streets of Dublin, I feel like my legs are almost weighed down now that we're here.

"I can't move that fast." The next thing I know, I'm being swung up into his strong arms. "Finn!" I exclaim just before his mouth crashes down.

With his lips still on mine, our kisses growing more frantic by the moment, we reach my door. Lowered down, I spin around and fumble with the card to open the lock. As soon as I manage it, Finn is nudging me through. Seconds later, my bag is flying through the air. I watch it land over Finn's shoulder as he hauls me off in the direction of the bedroom.

Sliding down off his shoulder is more erotic than any touch in my memory. Slowly, Finn lowers me inch by inch until our bodies align before his diabolical lips descend. Within moments, my dress is flung aside, and I manage to tear off his jacket and shirt, the sound of the buttons popping causing a rush of wetness between my legs.

Finn moans when he touches the scraps of lace I have on beneath my dress. "I haven't found a moment's peace since you."

What? "That's not possible," I breathe as we fall onto the bed.

"Later," he pleads as his wide chest lowers onto me. My fingers scrape along his back uncertainly, the need to touch him warring with the knowledge I'll be broken if I do.

"Touch me. Make a memory with me for when we're not together," he rasps.

Those words break what's left of my soul, my reservations. Because I need to revel here in this world with Finn.

Rolling us both, he makes quick work of his belt and slacks, shucking off everything after tossing his wallet near my head. Seconds later, I rise above him to look my fill.

"You still take my breath away," I whisper. It wasn't his looks that first drew me to him; it was his mind. The time we spent arguing in class where all the other voices fell away. Then one day I got lost looking at his full lips. And I blushed to the roots of my hair.

His face might have a few lines on it, some silver through his black hair now, but he's still the man I handed my heart to. Bending over, I place my lips over on his chest. Then I moan when his hands slide down my spine, releasing my bra, before cupping my breast, teasing the nipples. "And you give me life, Jenna." It sounds like a vow.

If only I could believe him.

I brush my now bare nipples against his hair-roughened chest. "God, Finn. Feels so good."

He rolls us both over, powerful muscles flexing. There's a crinkle of a wrapper, a pause, before there's nothing but the feel of our bodies as his thick cock nudges against my folds. Slowly, his erection stretches me until he's fully lodged inside of me.

"So bloody perfect. I..." But I don't want to ruin this with words. So, I arch my hips and capture his lips at the same time. I moan in pleasure, in pain, as he begins to thrust inside me.

I'm not sure if I remember to breathe as I allow my body to communicate everything I would never dare to say: *I miss you. I don't know what I did wrong. I still love you.* And I feel the conflict in his as he kisses me, hips pistoning steadily, so hard and thick inside me.

"Don't stop," I beg, needing desperately to finish this story once and for all so I can move on once our climax comes.

A rough growl next to my ear intensifies my own pleasure. Tighter and tighter, with each hard thrust until I begin quivering around him. He pushes deep inside me as he rides out his own orgasm.

As I drift off to sleep, tears saturate my pillow.

I scrunch my nose as it's being tickled with the ends of my hair. "Go'way," I mumble.

"Not until we talk, *mo chroí*. It's long past due." I freeze when I hear Finn's dark voice in my ear. Rolling over, I find him stretched out next to me, dressed in only his slacks.

"You're still here?" I ask wildly.

His face hardens at the question. "And that's one of the things we'll be discussing. Best be putting on a robe before I tumble you back against these sheets, Jenna."

Quickly, I slip from the bed and head into the bath. Giving myself a moment, I clean up before reaching for one of the robes. Entering the bedroom, I find Finn sitting on the edge of the bed, fingers laced behind the back of his head. My heart twists painfully, but I begin. "You didn't have to stay…"

He's on his feet in a flash. "You're going to let me explain, damn you," he roars.

His temper sparks my own. "I'm not the one who ran!" I yell.

That calms him. "I was a fool, and I paid the price."

"What price?" I ask bitterly.

"I didn't have you," he says simply. He makes his way toward me, but I hold up a hand to stop him.

"Don't. If you don't mean this, then just leave." I can't stop the fiery track of tears from flowing down my cheeks.

"I thought I was giving you a life," he says hoarsely.

"You gave me nothing I couldn't have had with you," I fling back. "And it's nothing I won't have once you're gone."

He flinches. "Don't you understand? I had to set you free."

"To do what, Finn? To live without you?"

He holds my gaze. "If that's what was meant to be, then yes."

My heart stops in my chest. "What are you saying?" I whisper.

He sidles up next to me and slips his fingers inside my robe. Fingers against my heart, he rasps, "I had to let you chase the world so if you came back, I knew you'd stay. So, I knew this would beat for me and not yearn for something else. You were so young…"

"And you were an idiot!" I shout. Shocking him, I shove Finn back at least a foot. "I traveled the world because I couldn't have the one piece of it I wanted."

"What's that?" The words are dragged from him.

I bare my soul to him. "You. All I wanted was you."

"Christ, I'm a stupid feck."

"If that means you're an idiot, I agree," I grumble as he pulls me close to his heart.

"My *seanmháthair* will wholeheartedly agree."

Tipping my head back, I ask, "What does that mean?"

"My grandmother. For what it's worth, she said that not long after I came home."

Home. Suddenly, my eyes grow wide. "Finn, I'm expected home in..."

"I know."

Eyes narrowing, I ask, "How?"

"Maura is very engaging, is she not? She asked your Emily where to send you thank-you flowers when you left here. So, tell me, *mo chroí*, would you like a visitor after the wedding?"

Even though it feels like all my wishes are coming true, I cautiously say, "Let's get through the wedding first."

Tugging me back toward the bed by the robe's belt, Finn agrees. "Of course."

"And what does '*mo chroí*'"—I massacre the pronunciation— "mean anyway?"

Tugging me back down on top of him, he cups my face in his hands before he whispers, "My heart."

Shit. With a sigh, I weaken. "If this happens, I just hope you're ready to meet my family. Some of them can be...protective." I think of Caleb, Keene, and Colby briefly, wincing, before Finn distracts me.

"We'll talk about them more. Later."

"Later," I murmur. Then I press my lips against his.

7

JENNA

An empty classroom in Connecticut, the crowded streets of Dublin. It doesn't matter. Regardless of where I am, Finn O'Roarke's lips on mine wipe every rational thought from my brain.

I slip from the bed the following morning where he's sprawled out and move into the sitting room to think since I can't manage to do it next to him.

There's a part of me that's elated the feelings between us still crackle like the summer heat lightning over the lake on my family's farm back in Connecticut, whereas the young woman devastated by his callous words is shivering, terrified of it all happening again. "What's to say this isn't a load of complete crap?" I whisper aloud.

"You have to trust me, Jenna. And I have to put my faith in you."

I whirl around to find Finn lounging in the doorway connecting the two rooms, a concerned expression on his face. "I thought you were asleep."

"I was until you moved. It was the most peaceful rest I've had in ages." He crosses the room until he's next to me. "But that's obviously not the case for you. Would you rather I leave, Jenna?"

The "No!" that escapes my lips is impassioned. It also points out very clearly what organ is ruling my decisions—my heart—because obviously my head is going to fight me the whole way. I lift a hand and lay it on his bare chest, my fingers nestling through the sprinkling of hair until I can feel the *thump, thump* of his heart against my palm. "I need time, Finn. I'm different from the girl who was in love with you."

A look of such pain crosses his face when I say those words, I want to take them back, but I refuse to hide any part of myself. He lays his hand over mine. "I know, Jenna. And I want to get to know the woman you've become. We can build on wishes and dreams, yes. But it's reality I want from you. Tell me what you need and I'll give it to you."

"Time." The word pops out of my mouth before I can stop it. His head rears back as if I've slapped him. I can understand his reaction; we've been separated for five years and I'm asking for more time alone. "I just need a few hours, Finn. I have some business calls to make, and I can use that time to wrap my head around all of this."

He leans down and presses a kiss on my lips. "How about you do what you need to and we get together later?"

Relief floods my system. "That sounds perfect."

He brushes his hand through my hair before heading into the bedroom. A few minutes later, Finn comes back to let me know he'll call me later.

I tell him honestly as I walk him to the door, "I look forward to it."

But once I close the door behind him, I worry aloud, "Now what am I supposed to do other than worry all day?"

Deciding that showering and changing is a good place to start, I make my way into the bathroom. But I can't help but stop and let my eyes linger over the wrecked bed and recall every delicious memory.

A few hours later, I've spoken with stores in Milan, Paris, and London, when my iPad bleeps with an incoming FaceTime call from my best friend, Lynne Bradbury. I immediately press Accept and shriek, "You are not going to believe what happened!"

"Get ready to tell me in about forty-five minutes. I'm coming your way! Uncle Ryan"—Lynne references my

 uncle-in-law through marriage, Ryan Lock-wood, one of the youngest billionaires in the world—"has thrown me on the jet. I'm sitting on the tarmac in Heathrow right now. I'm good to be in Dublin until I have to take off at three. That's a.m., since he's a closet sadist and scheduled us for a 4:00 a.m. conference call."

"What? Why?" I'm ecstatic Lynne is on her way here, but I'm confused as to why.

"Why did he schedule a call at that hour? He's trying to get some people from Dubai to donate money for the scholarship fund," Lynne explains.

"No, I guessed that. You've complained about meetings often enough. I mean, why the sudden trip to see me? Not that I'm not over the moon about it. I have so much to tell you."

There's a long pause where Lynne's bright blue eyes water. "Jenna, it's been nine years. Happy anniversary, babe."

And I feel the air leave my lungs just like they did outside of Cisco Brewery the day Em and I were in a life-or-death car wreck. I manage to say, "God, it is today."

"Em was going to fly over herself, but something came up with the kids. So, you get me. I hope that's okay?" Lynne gnaws down on her lip.

"It's better than okay. It's amazing."

"Are you sure?"

"Absolutely. Because now I can share all the details of seeing Professor Finn O'Roarke with you in person." I wait for her reaction.

"You ran into Professor O'Hell Yes? And I wasn't your first call seconds after you saw his face?" she screams. I'm fairly certain the crew in Ryan's cockpit have heard her.

"That might have been a bit awkward as after I helped his sister with her bridal dress fitting—she's one of Em's custom brides, by the way—and we managed to make it back to the hotel, I've barely been out of my bedroom. I can just see myself rolling off of him after round two and saying, 'Excuse me, Finn. I need to catch my bestie up that you're not a complete ass, though you can certainly still bounce quarters off of the supreme specimen of the one you have,'" I inform her dryly.

Lynne moans. "Oh, my God. You're cruel."

"Why?"

"Because it's been way too long since I've been near a man's ass in that way, and now I'm picturing you and Professor O'Roarke—again, I might add. It's downright cruel."

I burst out laughing. Then I remember I'm supposed to meet Finn later. "Want to catch up with our old prof?"

"Are you kidding? This is you giving me an anniversary gift instead of me giving one to you. Speaking of which, what do you want?"

I smile because we go through this every single year, and I say exactly the same thing. "Nothing but a hug from you. I'm just grateful for that and all of you in my life."

Lynne goes quiet. "And does that include Professor O'Roarke?"

I think. "Right now, yes. It does include Finn. But I'm not sure where it's going."

"Well, maybe we'll find out tonight. Okay, love. I'm being told to shut it down. I'll call you when we land."

"Love you, Lynne. Safe flight."

"Love you too, Jenna." She disconnects, leaving me with a crazy number of memories.

And something I know I need to do.

I pull up Spotify and send Em the link to "Head Above Water" by Avril Lavigne. It was the song Dani walked the runway to in Em's first Fashion Week show. The lyrics also perfectly match how she saved me emotionally as well as physically the summer before that occurred.

I type a quick note to accompany it. *Thank you for rescuing me in so many different ways. I love you — Jenna*

Then before I can do anything else, my room phone rings.

Knowing all of my calls are screened, I answer with a brisk, "Jenna Madison."

And when his sexy voice punches through the line, I wonder if I should pull back the email to Em and ask her to come rescue me one more time. I might need it.

8

FINN

P acing my hotel room, I ponder the timeline I have to convince Jenna we're meant to be together. Eight days.

Eight days to give her the parts of me I held back when she stood in front of me pleading for a chance before she flies back to her country. I have a scarce pittance of time to dive off the edge of the cliff I've wished for her on and do the impossible—let go of life's burdens to fly.

Is sacrificing lifelong agony of my heart worth it? And immediately I know the answer to be *without a doubt*. Nothing is worse than the punishment of oblivion I've suffered wondering if a simple word could have changed both our pasts.

Now, through the miracle of God or the machinations of my *seanáthair*, I've been granted the only selfish wish I've dared ask for. Sliding my phone from my pocket, I press a number and wait for the call to connect.

My sister immediately answers. "Finn, what is it? Is it *seanmháthair*?"

"No, *mo sicín beag*. I do need to ask a favor."

"Anything."

"Don't be so hasty. This one is rather large."

"Well, you won't know if you don't ask," she retorts.

I smile in spite of my nerves. After all, I'm about to invite a virtual stranger to my baby sister's wedding. I hedge. "I know it's last-minute, but I wanted to see..."

"If you could bring someone to my wedding?" The unfiltered amusement in Maura's voice catches me off guard as much as her words do.

"How did you know?" I demand.

"Grandmother warned me earlier. But even without it, I'd have to be completely daft not to feel the sparks between you. Still—" She clicks. "—Jenna must tell me her secret superpowers because I've never managed to get a man to perform the yank and pull before he kissed me. And here's my staid, serious big brother doing it after knowing her all but a few hours."

My cheeks flame as Maura recounts my behavior. "It's not completely like that."

"I saw the kiss, Finn." Maura's amusement is clear.

"No, I mean your assumption I've only known Jenna a few hours."

There's a prolonged silence on the other end of the line. Finally, Maura asks, "When did you meet her, Finn?"

I glance down at my watch to check the date. "Five years, six months, and two days ago, plus or minus a few hours for the time zone difference."

"She was your student?" my sister screeches.

"Where absolutely nothing happened until the moment she wasn't."

"Then where the bloody hell has she been all these years?"

"I pushed her away." My voice cracks as I dredge up the memory of Jenna standing before me, proudly recanting what love is supposed to be. "I thought it was for her own good."

Maura explicitly tells me what she feels about that. I scrub my hand over my face. "You can't call me anything I haven't called myself."

"And what would you have done if she showed up with a ring on her finger?"

"Wished her the happiness she deserves and loved her the rest of my life." My sister begins to sniff loudly. Immediately, I panic. "No, none of that, *mo sicín beag*. Now, back to my question. Can I—"

"You gave up everything for us, Finn." I begin to protest, but she cuts me off. "You gave up your dream job in America, your money, and I knew it. Knowing you gave up a chance at love, you could ask me for anything. A chair at my wedding reception is nothing. But there's one more thing."

My breath shudders out. "And that is?"

"*Seanmháthair* has already given me and Will our gift. We're building a bed-and-breakfast on the property. When that's done, she's moving in with us. This way we can both have our dreams, *deartháir*."

Instinctively, I put up a token protest, but it quickly subsides. I might need the shelter of my family if I can't convince Jenna of my heart in the next eight days. But if I can...

No, I can't think like that. That's asking too much when I feel I'm tempting fate already. Instead, I say, "We'll discuss it later."

"I love you, Finn."

"And I you, Maura."

"That, I've always known. Remember, love can see past mistakes to intent." And with that, she disconnects the call.

"God, I hope so." I need Jenna to understand fear and the worst timing imaginable kept me from her until I assumed she would want nothing to do with me.

And pray like hell there's some kernel of love still inside the woman who stood in front of me today.

After I end my call with Maura, I have the hotel operator ring Jenna's room. She answers with a brisk "Jenna Madison."

"Darling, hasn't anyone ever schooled you on proper protocol about traveling alone?"

"First, Professor, I'm not your darling. Second, yes. I have been."

"Then you know better than to answer your phone with your name," I chide her.

"I would agree, except the hotel announced who was calling. What do you need, Finn?" Her voice is exasperated.

You. But I barely catch myself before I say it so bluntly and drive her away before I've had a chance to win her back. "Dinner? I know a lovely pub nearby."

There's no hiding the smug amusement in her voice as she shoots me down. "No can do, Finn. I have plans."

"Lucky bloke." I think I've done an admirable job of tamping down my jealousy, but I begin to wonder when Jenna laughs.

"Wrong. Lucky me. In fact, Professor, you might know her."

"Her?" My mood lightens considerably.

"Yes. Lynne Bradbury."

My mind immediately calls up an image of a scarily brilliant brunette who often entered class with Jenna. I settle back against the sofa. "What is she doing these days?" I reach for the complimentary bubble water and pour some.

"Well, after she graduated from the London Business School, she took a job working for Lockwood Industries."

"Oh? Doing what?" I take a sip and let the bubbles swirl around my mouth. The bland, flavorless water picks up the lingering nuance of Jenna's taste.

But it comes flying out when Jenna declares smugly, "Directly reporting to Ryan Lockwood."

"Holy fecking hell. Good for her. I'd love to know how that came about."

Jenna hesitates. Then I hear a ping. "Well, you can ask her yourself. She said earlier you should join us for dinner, and her plane just landed."

A slow smile crosses my face. "What time should I meet you?"

"An hour in the lobby?"

"Right." My mind is reeling with questions. "I look forward to it."

A pause before her soft "Me too." Then the call is disconnected.

I immediately leap to my feet and fist-pump the air. It's not much, I admit to myself. But it's a start.

And I know as long as I don't lose hope, it is possible to recover my heart's vision.

So long as Jenna feels even a modicum of what I do for her after all this time.

9

JENNA

When I catch sight of Finn waiting in the lobby in well-worn jeans and a Henley, my legs wobble. And it has absolutely nothing to do with the fact I pushed my leg by wearing heels this morning to the appointment. As I get closer, his silver eyes rake over me from head to toe. A smile breaks out across his gorgeous face. "I do believe, *mo chroí*, this is the first time I've seen you in flats." His expression turns thoughtful.

Being reminded of my physical limitations rubs what little patience I have raw. "What? Am I suddenly unattractive to you because I'm not as tall as you expected? Sorry, not sorry, Professor. Now, if you will excuse me?" I turn away to get away from this man who unerringly triggers all of my emotions, good and bad.

Finn grabs a hold of my wrist as I'm mid-whirl, causing me to lose my balance. I tumble into his arms. Stiffening, I brace myself against his forearms to push myself back. I won't allow myself to feel the pain. I spent too many months flat on my back after the accident feeling breakable and terrified I'd never be whole again. Even when I physically recovered, I wasn't certain I was whole.

That is until this man skewered me the first time through the heart and mind with shards of silver, much the same way he is right now. "Jenna, are you all right?"

I brush the past that has both nothing and everything to do with Finn out of my mind. "Fine. I'm fine. Mind if we head out? I'm excited about seeing Lynne, and it makes me clumsy."

He holds out an arm. "Well. Let's get you there in one piece."

I slip my fingers in the crook of his arm to regain my balance, but it's a colossal mistake. The moment my fingers touch the skin at the crook of his elbow, I'm flung back into his classroom where I gripped just above this soft flesh, digging in with my nails as his cock sank inside of me slowly. Oh, so slowly.

My head snaps up to find his lips compressed, and I know he, too, is remembering. For a moment we're locked in the past, unable to do what he wants—take a step over the rocky gorge of our missing years to bring us safely to today. Together.

His breath releases, and I feel it ruffle the top of my hair. "The pub is a bit of a walk. Are you up for it?"

"Yes." Anything to get me away from where I am right now.

"Then let's be off." And holding my arm, Finn leads the way.

An hour later, I'm screaming with laughter at the dumbfounded expression on his face. After hugging me hello, Lynne declares, "Your uncle has a sadistic view of what he considers working hours."

"How do you think he became one of the youngest billionaires in the world?" I counter.

"I know he scheduled a meeting in the office at 4:00 a.m. which is why..." Lynne begins, but Finn interrupts.

"Back up just a moment, ladies. Lynne, it's a pleasure to see you again."

Lynne sticks out her hand, and Finn's eyebrows wing upward. "Professor. I must say it was a surprise, but it affords me the opportunity to thank you for grading my final exam such that it ensured my scholarship to business school."

"At least one of us got an A," I remark sweetly.

"You've yet to let me explain..." Finn starts, but I wave a hand carelessly as if his A minus didn't impact my graduating magma cum laude. Well, his changing the grading curve screwed me over, not that he hadn't already done that. I quickly flag a waiter down and order a glass of wine.

Lynne's wicked grin as she orders her favorite Irish whiskey does nothing to deter Finn's question. "Uncle?"

"It's more of an honorific thing. What do you want to drink?" I ask impatiently.

"Try telling that to the rest of the Freeman clan. You've been one of them since before they met you."

"True, but Ryan was a billionaire long before I became a part of it."

"Yes. And as he shoved me on the jet, he said to do this." Lynne reaches over and kisses my forehead. "He wants to know if one of his favorite nieces would like to fly home on the private plane instead of commercial."

"Umm, like he has to ask? Now let Finn order before you start bitching about your early meeting, and give Ryan a hug back from me."

Finn chokes. "Let me get this straight. Ryan Lockwood is your uncle?"

It's then I notice the paleness to his skin and feel a pinprick of pity. "Through marriage. It goes like this." And I quickly explain how my stepmother is related. "I'm incredibly blessed."

That's when Lynne becomes serious. "No, Jen, we are."

I flash her a warning look, which she ignores. Turning to the waiter, she asks, "Do you all have champagne?"

"Yes, ma'am."

"Great. We'll need that first."

"Are we celebrating something, Lynne?"

I try to stop her. "Lynne, I haven't..."

But either she doesn't hear me, or she ignores me. I'd bet my precious amaryllis earrings on the latter because she opens her mouth and immediately declares, "Absolutely. It's been nine years today since the day Jenna almost died. Em and her father would be sitting right here if she was home."

"Died?" Finn's voice echoes hollowly. He turns me toward him before cupping my cheek. "How?"

"Not tonight, okay?" The words slip out of my lips. My lips curve slightly. "I don't need this, but they do."

He tips my face upward, and the world diminishes to the silver glimmer in his eyes. "I can appreciate that." Brushing a soft kiss on my lips that has Lynne sighing dramatically, he calls out to the waiter, "A pint and a shot of your finest whiskey."

"Yes, sir." The waiter leaves our pub table, and Finn opens his mouth when over the din of the crowd, his name is called.

"Finn! Finn! Get that luscious face over here!" And before I can move, a voluptuous blonde is wedging herself between me and Finn to grab both of his cheeks and tug his face down to be kissed firmly on the mouth.

And I feel the heat rise in my face as I silently fume when the man whom I took inside my body doesn't protest but instead wraps his arms around the woman and hugs her tightly.

"Well, this certainly puts an interesting twist on things," Lynne leans over to murmur just as the waiter arrives back with our drinks.

"I'm debating whether to bash her or him upside the head with the champagne," I enunciate quite clearly. The waiter's head snaps up from where he'd been struggling to uncork the bottle. "That or grabbing our waiter..."

"Brit," he supplies helpfully.

"...to give this world-class jackass a taste of his own medicine before I walk right out," I declare hotly.

Whether Finn hears me or Octopus Arms has had enough, he whirls her around to face me with an enormous smile on his face, only to be met with an infuriated woman. "Jenna, *mo chroí*..."

"Save your *mo chroí* crap for someone who's going to believe it, Finn. God, I can't believe you'd stand there right in front of me and kiss another—"

"Cousin. My first cousin, Rosalie—Rosie—O'Roarke. She just arrived back from studying at the Sorbonne, so you didn't meet her at the shop when Maura had her fitting."

My eyes narrow on the lovely woman, who's grinning at me. "You're all Grandmother is talking about, Jenna. Well, that and the dress your family designed for Maura." She tilts her head up to Finn and purses her lips. "When I get married, can I have a dress like Maura's?"

"You all are going to drive me back into the poor house!" Finn adds a few words, and Rosie replies in kind. Within seconds, they're arguing as fiercely as they were adoring one another.

Absentmindedly, I beseech Lynne, "Pass me my drink."

She does, and we tap glasses before we settle in to watch Professor Finn O'Roarke lose his cool with a girl I can now easily estimate at younger than I was when I met him. I feel a jab in my arm. I glare at Lynne before I realize she's passing the bar nuts. Taking a handful, I mumble around them. "She's going to wear him down."

"No way. Em's dresses cost a fortune."

I take a sip of wine and admire the way Finn's trying to stand strong, but his heart is right there—just like it was last night when he convinced me to take a chance on him for the next eight days. "You can see it as he looks at her. He treasures her."

Lynne chews and swallows. "He looks at you the same way but with this intensity. Why didn't we notice it before?"

Blindly, I reach over and jab my hand into the nut bowl. "I don't know."

"What do you know, Jenna?"

"That I have to see this through." Giving up the thought of eating, I whirl around and face my best friend. "I wished for this chance for so many years, I can't just throw it away."

"And if it's not what you hoped for?" Lynne asks cautiously.

I cast a glance at the fighting cousins. What if Finn O'Roarke isn't the man I've been wishing for? "Then I'll keep wishing. But I'll know, won't I?"

"That you will." We tap glasses again just in time to hear Rosie call out, "See you at the wedding, Jenna!"

Finn grabs the first drink nearest him and downs it in a few gulps. I casually ask, "So, I presume Em will be making another dress for a member of the O'Roarke family?"

Finn shoots me a filthy look before his eye notices the champagne. "We'll talk about that later. Tonight, we need to celebrate something special. You."

"I honestly don't know what to say."

"Then don't say anything. Let me." Finn hands us each a flute. "Jenna, you make the world more special for being in it. Despite the trials you've endured, I hope your wishes coming true balance it out."

We clink glasses, and Lynne pronounces, "The man has a way with words."

That's what I'm afraid of, I think as my eyes meet Finn's over the rim of the glass.

"I's got to take a wizzle dizzle," Finn announces with some pride.

Lynne chokes on her whiskey. "Excuse me?"

"A wizzle dizzle," he slurs. "What's wrong with that?"

"Finn, you're sloshed," I pronounce.

"Completely langers," he agrees, not without a touch of pride. "Haven't done this in a... Hey, boy!" he shouts at a passing waiter.

Lynne's drink must burn as she snorts it out of her nose. I hand her a handful of napkins and stifle my laughter as Finn tries to have a conversation about soccer with the waiter. No, I mentally correct myself, it's football, and I'd better remember that before the hot mess in front of me takes me to task.

"Musha faith." He holds out his hand, and the waiter does some kind of complicated handshake before he staggers off to what I can only presume is the men's room.

Three seconds later, we're a giggling mess.

Lynne regains her voice first. "Is this some kind of alternate universe where Professor O'Hell Yes just became a frat boy?"

I lift my wine to my lips and drink deeply. "I'm beginning to think so, yes."

"It's fabulous. I'm calling Ryan to quit. I can work with you, right?"

Before I can answer, Finn's arm drapes heavily around my waist. "*Mo chroí*, I'm completely rat-arsed."

"If that means what I think it does, we noticed." Concerned, despite my amusement, I twist in his arms and tip my face back so I can take stock. "Lynne, I might need your help getting him into a taxi."

She waves my request off. "I have a car. I just need to call the driver."

Even though I'm grateful, I can't help but tease her, "You are getting way too used to the perks of working for Lockwood Industries —drivers, private jets, five-star accommodations. What are you going to do if it all goes away?"

"I don't know. I guess I'll find out soon enough." Her words are calm, but her eyes are anything but.

Finn has dropped his head to my shoulder. I figure he must have started to fall asleep because he jerks his head back with a snap when I screech, "What do you mean?"

"I mean, I have an opportunity to take a job with Bristol Brogan-Houde. You've heard me mention her—the Queen of Wall Street."

"Only like a million times. She's your freaking idol, Lynne." I want to race around the table and hug my best friend, but I have a dead weight in my arms.

She knows this and is outright laughing at me. "You can hug on me once we dump Professor O'Hell Yes in his suite."

I shoot her a look of horror. "I can't leave him in this condition. What if he chokes on his own vomit or some shit?"

"What if?" Lynne murmurs. "What do you want to do with him, then?"

"We'll just bring him back to my suite. He can sleep it off on the couch."

Lynne nods somberly. "That's a perfect idea."

I struggle a bit under Finn, who I think is beginning to snore. "Can we do it soon? He's getting awfully heavy."

"One would think you would be used to that weight. I mean, it's not like you haven't had him on top of you a few times to adjust to the man's form," Lynne remarks as she pushes buttons on her phone.

My eyes water, and it's not due to the alcohol stench emanating off Finn. It's because since the summer I almost died, this amazing woman gave me purpose. "I love you." Lynne's head snaps my way, and her big blue eyes go wide. "Thank you for coming all this way just to be with me."

"I love you too. And this is what family does." A wry smile crosses her face as she stands and walks around the table in a custom-made dress Em designed for her the summer we met. "Yours taught me that. Now, let's get you both back to your hotel so I can go to work."

10

FINN

The streaming light wakes me. "I made a right bag of that."

I must be in Hell because Jenna replies, "Are you still drunk, because I'm still trying to look up all the Irish you used last night. My favorite was the way you talked about going to the bathroom."

I groan. "Tell me I'm in the middle of a nightmare."

Much too cheerfully in my estimation, she approaches, looking younger than her twenty-five years in bare feet and jeans with her hair twisted up in a loose knot. She holds out a glass of water and a small travel-size bottle of medicine. Gratefully, I accept both, quickly swallowing the tablets before I ask, "Lynne got off all right?"

Jenna sits down on the table across from me. "She was also very disappointed that I wouldn't completely undress you in front of her. Claimed it was a betrayal to every female who fantasized about 'your luscious body' and was distracted by it when they attended your lectures. I told her to kiss my ass. She did. You missed quite a show in your passed-out state, Finn."

I grin as vague memories of Jenna cursing me for having such large feet and wearing boots just to annoy the piss out of her flash into my mind. "I'm sure I did."

She twists her fingers back and forth. "Why did you get so obliterated?"

I lay my hand on top of hers. "I'm Irish, Jenna. We're a superstitious lot."

"Okay." She draws out the word.

"I'd already lost you—I thought it was once. Hearing about your brush with death made me realize it was actually twice."

Her face softens. "I was sixteen, Finn. It was long before I met you." She flips her hand under mine so our fingers can twine together.

I shake my head. "Despite the number of years I worked to escape my roots, they're a part of me. I believe deeply in the power of three; it's sacred in ancient Celtic mythology and religion. There's many folklore passed down through the generations, including my own family. Did you know the human soul is comprised of three layers?" She shakes her head. "Well, it is. It becomes imperative when the soul is tied so closely to love, *mo chroí*. What if this is our last chance to get things right?" I swing my legs over so I'm sitting up and facing her.

Her breath catches. I lay my hands on her knees. "And I believe this, Jenna. If it's not, how can you account for the fact first it was your body that was hurt? Then your mind, by my own actions—damn me. But I swear to you, I will not break your spirit."

She still hasn't said a word but slowly rises to her feet. Much like the Wiccan goddesses that are as common here as the Christian ones, Jenna's eyes blaze down at me. "Do you think I would give you the chance? What happened to me wasn't due to fate but a man's carelessness—both times."

I wince at her choice of words but don't speak. "I was driving my stepmother due to her own grief, and we were hit head-on by a drunk driver. I suffered horribly. And without a thought to her own welfare, Emily breathed life back into me in those moments when my brain refused to function correctly. I also shattered my ankle..."

"And you wear those heels?" I ask incredulously.

"It's my life, Finn! If I choose to wear heels, I'll pay the price. I pay the price for every decision I've ever made. Just like I did when I chose to accept you into my arms, my body, my damn soul five years ago. But despite having slept with you again, despite still having feelings for you, it will be *my* decision if you'll get that last piece of my soul you claim is on the line. Me. This isn't a star-crossed love like your Tristan and Isolde. This is me and you, buddy." Jenna scoots around me and storms over to the window.

I push to my feet and follow her. "I didn't mean to imply otherwise."

"Then what did you mean, Finn?" Fatigue fills her voice.

I pull her back against me and try to think of an appropriate analogy. "Do you remember when you would be working on a paper and there's this urgency to get it completed so you could relax, celebrate?"

Her expression is amused. "Actually, I do. I had this monster of a professor for International Marketing my senior year of college. He was a total beast."

I pinch her arse. "Real cute."

"But yes, I understand. Em feels the same way right before a show. There's an impending sense of no matter how much effort you put into it, at the eleventh hour, something's going to happen." She twists around to face me. "I understand."

I pull her close and just hold her for a moment. Then Jenna starts squirming. I frown. "What is it?"

"I hate to be blunt about it, but Finn? You kind of still smell like the pub."

I roar with laughter before I press a smacking kiss to her cheek. Her nose scrunches up adorably. "How about I go clean up and then we find something to do?"

"Perfect." I start to move away. "Wait, Finn? I'm going to get ready. Let me just give you my spare key to let yourself back in."

"Now there's a way to make sure I hurry, *mo chroí*."

Jenna's still laughing as I slip out of her room to head down the hall toward my own.

I'm overjoyed to find her still laughing when I reenter her suite an hour later. "Really, Mom. I had a good time with Lynne." I can barely hear another female voice as I move out of

 the foyer into the main room. Knocking on the doorjamb, I make my presence known.

Jenna waves me in. "Actually, Mom, there's someone I want you to meet. Finn, come here a moment."

My heart skips a beat as I hear a woman's voice call out, "Jenna, honey? You met someone?"

"Actually, Mom, I've known him quite a while. The timing just never worked out before."

"Well, isn't that lovely," the voice, an older version of Jenna's, exclaims.

"Mom, this is Finn O'Roarke. I knew him when I was back in college. Finn, my mother, Michelle."

I crouch next to where Jenna's sitting. "Hello, Ms...." My eyes widen at Jenna. What the bloody hell do I call her mother? I can't very well address her as Michelle, can I?

Apparently, I can. "Just make it Michelle, Finn. I was Mrs. Madison for a number of years. But now that Em's last name is Freeman-Madison and I'm remarried to Eric, it'd be all kinds of confusing." There's an amusement on her face that's contagious.

"Michelle. It's a pleasure to meet a member of Jenna's family outside of Lynne."

"See what I mean, Mom?" Jenna crosses her arms over her chest and smiles smugly at me.

"I do, honey." Both women laugh.

"What?" I ask warily.

"Nothing," Jenna purrs, raising every hair on my body in latent male fear. I eye her long hair and debate if I can muzzle her with it as she wraps up her coded conversation with her mother.

"I think you're going to pay for this one, Jenna. Finn is plotting your murder," Michelle observes astutely.

Jenna shrugs as if it makes no never mind to her. I decide two can play at this game. "And I had such a lovely surprise planned for her today."

Jenna mean mugs me while Michelle laughs delightedly. "He's got your number, baby. I'll leave you two to fight it out. Jenna, your father and Em asked Eric and me to join the family at the farm for the night you land. Apparently there's going to be a dinner?"

"I'm not surprised. Any excuse for the family to dance on tables." My jaw unhinges at the unusual comment. But it doesn't unnerve Michelle in the slightest.

"That's what Em yelled in the background. She was picking out music."

Jenna claps her hands together. "No one had better take my spot on the bar."

"All I have to say is you're going to have to be lonely up there by yourself if Lynne won't be home," Michelle warns.

"Oh, come on, Mom. Join me. Just shake it like you own it. You'll do fine."

"And that's my cue to go. Goodbye, Jenna. I love you. Nice to meet you, Finn." And Michelle's image disappears from the screen.

"Was she serious?"

"That it was nice to meet you? I'm sure she was. I've never introduced her to anyone I've ever dated."

"Wait, I meant the dancing on a bar at a farm, but let's talk about that last comment first. What do you mean you've never introduced your mother to anyone you've dated?"

"Where are we going?" Jenna demands.

I pull her to her feet and kiss her. "Go grab whatever you need to walk."

She grabs a small backpack from the chair and shoves her wallet deep inside with a light sweater and her phone. "I'm ready."

"Then decide what you'd like to do and we're off."

Her eyes narrow. "You didn't have a thing planned, did you?"

"I actually do, but it doesn't start for a few hours. So, the morning is yours." I loop my arms around her and tug her to me. "Anything, Jenna. Just name it."

"You know what I'd really like to do," Jenna says thoughtfully.

"What's that?" I imagine she's going to want to take in one of the many fairs around the city, maybe a museum.

"Can we visit where you went to school?" she asks shyly. Her fingers reach up, and she begins to twirl them in the ends of my hair.

My mind completely blanks. "Excuse me?"

She leans forward, and her voice is serious as she explains. "Finn, I didn't just fall for your face all those years ago; it was your mind I fixated on first. I'd like to understand what helped shape it."

It takes a moment for her words to register because I'm stunned. Not because Jenna said them, but because they're so reflective of my own feelings for her. "I'd be honored to show you around my uni."

Jenna beams at me. "Do you think it will be a problem to walk around the campus?"

Briefly, I think of Trinity University's infamous library and hope there's not a tour there when I show it to Jenna. I want to bring her up into the galley and show her where I spent hours studying to learn about the historical perspective of business. Smiling slowly as I shake my head, I eagerly anticipate her telling me later the hours I spent there were complete rubbish.

And this time I can do exactly what I wanted to all those years ago —kiss her madly to stop her argument.

"Trinity University, recognized internationally for research expertise in applied economics, afforded me the chance to intensely study theoretical as well as applied economics before I went on and applied for my doctorate. I found I had a talent for modeling of economies and applying the models' global imbalances," I inform Jenna as we walk toward my alma mater.

"Why teaching? Why didn't you go into the corporate world?" she probes.

I stop and pull her into my arms. "I did my time in that never-ending cesspool. And I was utterly miserable. Worked for five years in corporate finance for a large financial firm before deciding to go back for my doctorate. You see, Jenna, I still *had* to be immersed in the subject I loved, but I didn't have to put in eighty-to-one-hundred-hour workweeks just to meet expectations. I was incredibly happy."

Her face clouds. "Then, we happened and you left."

"No. Jenna. That's not it at all." I pull her out of the way of some people and up against a stone wall. "Something happened shortly after you left that day."

"What?" I don't blame her for her guarded tone.

"I received a call from Maura. My grandfather had died. I flew home immediately." I open my mouth to say more, but I find my arms suddenly filled with Jenna.

"I'm so sorry. So incredibly sorry. You were close."

"I suppose, in a way more than anything you'd find inside these walls, he made me the man I am."

Jenna doesn't say a word, just holds on and smooths her hand up and down my back. I bury my face in her hair. It isn't until I taste the salt against my lips do I realize scalding tears are dripping out of my eyes. Finally, I'm able to let loose some of the pressure of my grandfather's loss.

I'm not certain how long we stand there, but when I speak again, it's to tell her, "After I could think again, I was going to try to contact you, but what could I say? I was such an arse, Jenna. And every time I tried to compose an email, it sounded so ridiculously stupid. Then, the farm was in trouble and..."

She pulls back with a frown. "Our farm was never in trouble, Finn."

A tickle of her conversation with her mother nudges at me. "Your farm? I meant mine, ours. It's been in the family for five generations."

Shadows are washed away by delight. "I meant the Freeman farm, Finn. It's where I live when I'm not traveling."

Another shared link. Another bond. "I have to go pick up my grandmother in a few days, just before the wedding. Would you like to ride with me? See the farm?"

She links her arm in mine. "Absolutely. But first, I have this odd desire to know all about the Finn O'Roarke who drove all the coeds mad with desire."

I tug her close before we start walking toward Stephen's Green. "There weren't that many."

Jenna outright laughs in my face. "Maybe not that you acted on, but let me tell you, Professor, there were plenty that fantasized. And I want to see how it all began."

"Well, then, do you want the tour that includes the underground wine cellar or not?" I get into the spirit of things.

"Oh, I think that's a must, don't you?"

I tug her closer as we walk around the square. "As long as it's with you, it is."

11

FINN

"Tired?" I ask Jenna as we depart campus where she managed to kiss me senseless in "the stacks" just "because I can, Finn. I mean, look at this place." She spun around the famed legal deposit library. "It's glorious."

"So are you," I murmured before taking her mouth again.

"How would you feel about a small festival?"

"Is there shopping and food?"

"And singing as well, I imagine."

"Then I feel very warmly about this as I've yet to purchase anything for my family. Let's go."

An hour later, Jenna and I are sharing a basket of chips with a healthy dose of salt and vinegar when I finally ask about her relationship with her mother and stepmother as she's undoubtedly close to both of them. "Mom was absent for most of my life. She was too busy trying to make up—to herself—for cheating on Dad and abandoning me when I was a baby."

I'd just been about to shove another chip into my mouth, but it drops to the ground unnoticed. "Excuse me?"

Jenna nods. "I imagine you can understand that as a result, I've never put my heart completely out there except with a couple of close family members—particularly my dad and my cousin, Danielle." She pauses and gives me a long look.

"That's nice. Are you and Danielle close in age?"

Jenna starts to giggle. "For real, Finn?"

"What? So you have a cousin named Danielle? So, what? Is there something special about that?"

Jenna lifts my pint from my hands and takes a sip. "I think I'll hold on to this. Finn, what's my name?"

"Jenna," I reply like she's daft.

"My full name."

"Jenna Madi...oh shit." I grab my beer back and begin drinking. When it's about halfway done, I whisper loudly, "Are you trying to say your cousin is *the* Danielle Ma—"

She slaps her hand over my mouth. "Yep. I was living in her house when I met Em. Em's her exclusive clothing designer."

"Whoa." It's a lot to take in. But even though I see the resemblance in the long blonde hair, the shape of the eyes, and the cheekbones, I declare, "She may be more striking, but you're naturally prettier."

Jenna flushes. "Charmer. That's because she's married to the hottest country musician. Ever."

"Now *that* causes my head to swoon."

"You're Irish. You like music."

"That doesn't mean anything. I'm in shock. You're related to..."

"Please don't go gaga over Brendan. It was bad enough Lynne had a life-size poster of him on her wall when we met. I thought the day she met him she might faint."

I roar with laughter. "How old were you?"

"We were both sixteen." Jenna takes my beer back and takes a sip. "Meanwhile, I was too busy crushing on Em's soon-to-be brother-in-law. He's delicious."

"You realize I'm devastated I'm not the first older man to catch your eye, darling."

"I can tell." We both break up laughing. I lay the chips to the side before taking her hand. "I'm sorry things were rough with your mother."

"I'm sorry they were rougher for my dad. I was a handful. I got busted for drugs at one point."

Now that shocks me. "You?"

She nods. "They let me off with a warning, but Dad completely uprooted our life to get me away from what he considered a bad influence. It turns out it was the best thing that could have happened to us."

"Except you almost died," I whisper.

"Finn, yes. I almost died, but look what I gained." She twists on the bench to face me. "I met Lynne. I met Em and the rest of the Freemans. So did Dad, and he fell in love—the kind of love that forgives anything. The kind that you can believe in for always. I was surrounded by people who fought for me, for my dreams. Yes, for a while I was physically fragile, but inside? I felt unbreakable."

"Until that day in my classroom." I fling my napkin to the side.

"Yes, until then. But even then, I became stronger as a result of it. I may not be the same girl who would have followed you around without question, but I'm the woman who's finding love all over again."

I drag my finger down her cheekbone. "And every moment I spend with you just makes my heart more certain it knows what it wants."

"What's that?" she asks breathlessly.

I lean forward and lay my lips on hers. "You."

For long moments, we just breathe in the essence of each other as our lips touch. With the music of a nearby fiddle, the sun filtering through the trees, it's almost magical. A moment that feels blessed. A wish come true. So, I risk all the progress I've made by whispering, "There will never be a moment throughout time when I won't be in love with you, Jenna."

She swallows hard and opens her mouth to speak. But I can't hear her say otherwise. Not right now. Instead, I just lay my finger across her lips. "I just needed for you to know that."

Jenna nods and turns her head to kiss the center of my palm, a soothing gesture. One I'll hold close.

But not as close as I would the words knowing she loved me as well. Still. Always.

12

JENNA

"I t's just a few days until the O'Roarke wedding," I remind Em over a FaceTime call.

"What do you have left to do?" Em's head is ducked as she takes notes on a pad.

"I was at the salon with Maura yesterday. The dress is perfect, of course." Em hums her pleasure. I go on. "Day-of assistance, including makeup. She has this ridiculously beautiful red hair that reminds me of Holly's."

"We should tie her down and shave it," Em mutters.

"The bride?" I gasp.

"Holly. I've always envied her hair. I wake up and your father has to look at a rat's nest. Holly wakes up and she's ready for a photo shoot." Em's head snaps up, and there's an evil gleam in them as she contemplates shaving her younger sister's hair—likely just for fun.

"Em, I can't stop a family war from thousands of miles away," I warn her.

"I wonder if Phil would..." she starts.

"*No!*" I shout just as the door to my suite opens. Finn pops his head around the corner, holding up two cups of to-go coffee. I nod desperately and hold out my hand. "Nothing that starts 'I wonder if Phil...' anything ends well, Em! What the hell is wrong with you?"

Em gives it two seconds before she bursts into gales of laughter. "Oh, Jenna. I'd be more inclined to shave Phil's head than Holly's. You should know better than that."

"Then why..."

"Consider that retribution from me and Dani hearing about the not really new man in your life when we had dinner with your mother yesterday. And as a result of having to sit on your cousin to prevent her from screaming in the middle of a restaurant, we ended up with an adorable mention in StellaNova. Not."

I groan. "I'm so sorry, Em. Things are happening so fast."

"I don't need all the details, sweetheart. I just want to know if you're happy so when the time comes, I can reassure your father."

My eyes drift upward from the little green dot and meet Finn's silver ones. "That's all you want to know? Am I happy?"

"For all of my children—and you know I consider you one of them, Jenna—that's all I've ever wanted for any of you."

My eyes still haven't left Finn's. "I've never been closer to the true happiness I've been taught to reach for than right now."

Finn's face intensifies with all the emotions he's feeling: passion, determination, and love. And even as each one is tattooed on my heart, I feel myself drawn upward. His lips brush lightly over mine. "*Mo chroí*," he whispers before letting me down back into my chair and moving away.

My eyes track his every movement, taking note of the way his tailored pants lovingly cup his rear when I hear Em ask, "Are you still planning on coming home after the wedding?"

My attention returns to her. "Right now, that's the plan."

Her perfectly groomed brows raise, asking me without words a million questions—none of which I have an answer for just yet. So, I just shrug helplessly. Her amused laughter rings out. "Michelle believes differently."

My lips curve. "And so do you, I take it."

"I've always believed in a lot of things when it comes to family,

Jenna. What are you and your professor's plans for today?" Finn whirls around, slack-jawed over Em's astuteness.

"We're heading to Waterford. I've never had the opportunity to go," I remind her.

"I should send you money to go shopping for me. The holidays are coming."

"And take away my ability to shop for the whole family at once? You're crazy, Em."

"One of the many reasons I've survived in this family. I'll pass along your love to everyone."

"Please do. Especially Dad, Jonas, and Talia."

"Always. Professor O'Roarke," Em calls out.

Finn jerks. "Yes, ma'am?"

Em's grinning like a lunatic, even as she uses the voice she typically scolds her brother with. "I'm not in the mood to clean up another broken heart anytime soon."

Before Finn can utter a single word, she winks at me and disconnects the line, leaving me grateful that the remarkable woman my father fell in love with healed not only my body but my mind when I needed it.

"Did your stepmother just call me out?" Finn's flabbergasted.

I close my iPad and place it to the side. "The Freemans are terribly protective of family, and none of them are discreet about hiding it. That includes the immediate family, spouses, cousins, and those of us they've adopted over the years."

Finn steps in front of me. "She knows about us?"

"Each of the members of my family has had a difficult path to love, Finn. They were worried about me. One night in Paris, Dani and Em supported me by being there when I finally let my emotions out. I wasn't fully living. They supported me and wanted to let me know they were there for me as they always have been."

"I owe them an enormous debt of gratitude, then. All I've ever wanted was for you to be happy, Jenna."

I rest my hands on his chest. "They'll make you pay for it."

His arms slip around my waist. "How's that?"

"That family dinner they're talking about? They're a regular thing. If this goes the distance and you attend one, you'll be on the hot seat, *Professor.*" I stress Finn's honorific much like Em just did.

His smile is slow and seductive. His head bends until his lips are a whisper away from mine. "Not if, Jenna. When. And I will take anything so long as I have you next to me."

My heart begins thumping wildly in my chest. Judging by the look on Finn's face, he knows how his words have affected me. But his words have always had a way of sneaking past my defenses. Now, I have to weigh them against his actions.

And right now that means shopping for things that will sparkle when they arrive back home.

"I can't believe you got us tickets for the factory tour!" I exclaim as we walk onto the retail floor of the House of Waterford.

"To be honest, I purchased them around the same time Maura commissioned her dress," Finn admits.

I stop dead. "You're kidding."

"Not at all. They're almost as impossible to come by as one of your family's designs. But I had hope, *mo chroí.*"

I lean up and have just pressed my lips to Finn's when I spy exactly what I want over his shoulder. "I'll be right back."

I wander in the direction of the champagne flutes until I find the design I hope I can have customized. Finn comes up next to me. "Did you find something that catches your eye?"

"I need to speak with a salesperson."

Finn twists his head and catches the eye of one. She comes over. "Hello. My name is Siobhan. How can I help you today?"

I lift the crystal flute. "First, do you have six sets of this flute in stock?"

"I'd have to check, but I believe we do."

"Excellent." I put the glass down and reach up to remove my earring. "Next, would it be possible to have each one engraved with this?" I hold out the earring I was given by the Freemans on the day of the *Promoter Quarterly* shoot on the palm of my hand.

Instead of taking it, Siobhan murmurs, "What a lovely design. If you don't mind waiting, I'll go get one of our engravers to speak with you personally."

"Thank you."

Siobhan excuses herself. Finn doesn't reach for my hand. Instead, he brushes my hair away from my other ear from behind. He remarks idly, "When I saw an article about you years ago, I felt compelled to research Amaryllis Events. The legend of Alteo and Amaryllis is on the site."

My voice is shaky when I reply, "I know."

"It holds magic, tragedy, and beauty, as so many stories about love do." Slowly, Finn turns me to face him. "And surprises me not at all you wear its symbol."

Tears fall from my eyes. "They gave it to me. When I most needed it, the family told me they were reminding me I was loved."

"And now you are doing the same. Regardless of the personal cost," Finn murmurs.

I nod, just as the engraver comes up. He slips on a white glove before asking to hold my earring. I appreciate the gesture. "Oh, this is lovely. Let's sit a moment so I can sketch." We're gestured to a small table off to the side.

When he places my earring on a crystal pad and turns it in a few directions, all I feel is comfort. It reminds me of cozy afternoons spent in Em's studio with my little sister cuddling up next to me. Inevitably, all of the family members make their way down there, including—my smile grows—Corinna with her delicious baked goods.

"What do you think, miss? I think this one"—he taps the third drawing—"will be the easiest to transfer onto the flutes you selected."

"Oh! Oh, it's perfect. Finn, don't you think so?"

I feel his lips press down on the crown of my head. "I'd hand out a box of tissues first, *mo chroí*. They're all going to be in tears."

The engraver hands me my earring back and clasps my hand. "Rath Dé ort." He nods at Finn before disappearing.

I slip my earring back in before asking, "What does that mean?"

It's Siobhan who translates. "'The Grace of God on you.' As Walter tends to be a bit of a boar, you made quite the impression. Now, if you don't mind coming with me for the more mundane matters?"

It takes about thirty minutes to fill out forms after chatting with Siobhan. I feel terrible for Finn, who must be bored senseless. But when it's done, I'm assured the six sets of flutes will arrive in plenty of time for the holidays. I hold out my hand. "Thank you, Siobhan."

"No, thank you, Jenna. Safe travels back to America." We shake, and I step out of her office with a much lighter heart and bank account.

Both are worth it.

Finn's reaching over the sales counter, accepting his own distinctive Waterford bag. I flash him a bright smile. "Doing some holiday shopping of your own?"

"Some shopping, yes. What say you we get something to eat? I'm famished." He wraps an arm around me before guiding me out of the store into the sunlight.

"I'd love it." But I stop in place and pull his head down and plant a long, slow kiss upon his lips.

It's a while before I let him come up for air. When I do, he's clearly taken aback. "Not that I'll ever mind you doing that—and feel free to encourage that emotion anytime—but what was that for?"

"For making a wish a long time ago and not giving up hope." I know I must have shocked him because he doesn't protest when I declare, "Oh, and I'm buying lunch."

"Yes. Where would you like to go?"

That's when I whisper in his ear, "Back to my room. We'll eat later."

It was a lot later. And by that time, Finn ordered half the menu, he was so hungry.

13

JENNA

"What I find fascinating is both our lives were influenced by people who live on farms," I inform Finn as we bump along the last part of the two-and-a-half-hour drive from Dublin to Burren in County Clare.

"I still can't picture you living on a farm, Jenna."

"The best time is first thing in the morning or as the sun sets. It depends on the season."

"There's a spot I can't wait to show you, *mo chroí*. Ever since I came back to Ireland, it's where I go to steady myself. It was my grandparents' place. Are there places on your farm like that?"

I nod, happiness bubbling up inside me as I pull up mental images of the daily chaos on the Freeman farm. "Yes. Behind Em's, Cassie's, and Phil's homes is this enormous lake. The main farm building also sits on it as well. Ali's home backs up to this gorgeous tree line; Corinna's and Holly's homes are against the edge of a brilliant wildflower field."

"Do you miss it?"

I open my mouth immediately to say yes but thoughtfully choose my words. "Yes and no. I miss the people every second of every day."

He downshifts. "That I appreciate."

"But I didn't grow up on the Freeman farm, though I would argue the most influential years of my life were spent on it."

"How did that come about?"

I start to answer, but my teeth jar just as Finn hits a bump in the road. He curses roundly, and I laugh freely. "Even though I met Em when I was sixteen, we didn't technically move there until after I graduated high school."

"After your accident?" Finn releases the stick shift and captures my hand.

"That's a part of it. A big part. There were some other factors..." Definitely not mine to share, I think ruefully. "But it resulted in Dad finishing out the school year—did I mention he's a music teacher?"

"No. Your father's an instructor as well?"

"He does a lot more than that; he actually helps Brendan compose his songs—something I didn't find out until after I graduated college."

Finn laughs. "I can't imagine why he didn't share that bit of knowledge."

"I can't either." I manage a reasonable pout for all of two seconds. We both laugh, and I return to the original story. "Anyway, after Dad finished out his term and I graduated, we moved there. It wasn't long before Dad and Em married, though we spent quite a bit of time there before that. I spent every summer since I was sixteen interning with Amaryllis Events; it was all I ever wanted to do." I laugh softly, recalling the family's infamous battles—Em's threats during Fashion Week, Corinna's flinging of food, and everyone threatening Phil. Lord, how they've mellowed over the years. "When I first signed on, I realize I didn't really have a marketing plan insomuch as I was P. T. Barnum corralling a circus."

Finn laughs uproariously. "That's the way it is with most businesses, *mo chroí.*"

Huh. Maybe I did learn something from Finn after all. I begin to giggle.

"What's so amusing?"

I recount my thoughts. "Right after we saw each other again, you said you were impressed with the way I ran my marketing campaign when really it was something you taught me."

Finn flashes me a quick grin before he drops my hand to navigate a sharp turn. Then, we make our approach toward the brown thatched roof covering cream walls. Beyond it, I see just off the edge of the world. It's spectacular. I blurt out the first thought that pops into my mind. "Why would Maura not want to get married here?"

Finn idles his car before leaning over and pressing his lips against mine. Lingering over the kiss, he murmurs, "Be sure to mention that to *seanmháthair*. I'm sure she'll give you the answer."

"Because she's going to live here the rest of her life. She wanted a different memory," Finn's grandmother explains after dinner when I finally ask her the question.

"Listen, Hannah, even if I was going to spend the rest of my days here, I'm still not certain I wouldn't want to get married right at the top of that flat rock. Just as the sun was setting." My voice gets dreamy. "Where I could make a wish all my days would be as happy as the one ending."

Finn and Hannah exchange smiles. Then she stands and holds out her arm. "Jenna, would you make this old woman happy and walk with me?"

"Absolutely."

Hannah is a delight. She has no qualms about showering him with love and blistering his ears when she feels he deserves it. When I asked if she was taking applications for adopted granddaughters, she shot me an ageless, amused look. "You know exactly how to become a member of this clan, Jenna. Don't be as daft as this one."

Finn grumbles something unintelligible under his breath.

Now, watching the sun beginning to set, her arm lightly clutching mine as we wander through a well-worn path, we climb the stone stairs until we reach the plateau at the top. My breath backs up in my throat as I move to what feels like the edge of forever. "It's breathtaking."

I'm absorbed in the beauty until Hannah makes her way next to me. Her murmured words over the rush of the wind undo me completely. "It's where Finn's grandfather and I were married."

"Oh, Hannah." Tears well in my eyes. "Finn has mentioned how much he was an influence on his life."

She confirms. "He was. And he'd have been as furious as I was if Finn stood just where you are now and admitted he carelessly threw away love. I considered shoving him over the edge."

Despite the ache her words cause, I can so easily picture this matriarch doing just that. I can't help but ask, "When did he do such a stupid thing? When he was a young man?"

"If he was some young welp, I'd have had him thrashed for wasting precious time. No, Jenna. It was after he saw your face in a magazine. That's when he finally broke down and told me the full story about his young student in America. Though long before that, he had already told me about the woman whose love he ran from."

"That was years ago." I can't keep the note of incredulity from my voice, nor the pain when I recall the number of stars I wished for some sign Finn O'Roarke was thinking of me. And now to find he not only had been thinking of me but held the same emotions churning inside of him that have been eating away the core of my heart? I inhale sharply and turn away.

But she's not done. "When I saw the way his eyes followed you at the salon, I knew immediately who you were. Finn is a great deal like his grandfather, loyal and true."

I make a sound that's an inhale conjoined with a sob. Yes, while I tried to forget him, us, Finn remained steadfast to the feelings we created together. I swipe my hand beneath my eyes to mop up the tears dripping down my face. "So many nights, I prayed for a man— any man—to relieve me of what I was feeling."

"Why?"

"Oh, Hannah. I've asked myself that very question about your grandson so many times. Why did he hurt me? Why did he push me away? Why is he here persistently trying to push his way back into my life? Why am I bracing myself for him shoving me out of his life again?" The last is shouted with all of the pain I've held in since I stood in Professor Finn O'Roarke's classroom over five years ago.

That's when I catch sight of him reaching the pinnacle of the stone stairs. And on his face is every emotion I've just released. I thought I was flinging my fear toward the stars to rid myself of it. I never intended for it to be targeted at the man I've spent years wishing for. Determined, I race past Hannah and toward Finn.

His face loses its haggard expression as I approach across the stone flat. But it quickly firms into the man I've spent years dreaming of as I approach. He steps off the stairs just as I reach him. I slap my hands against his chest. "Why? Why now?"

His arms clasp mine. He snarls, "Because I've been begging anyone who would listen for you since the first time I looked at you."

"You've what?" I'm so stunned, I stumble, but Finn's arms tighten around me.

"It started with that mind of yours, that incredibly brilliant mind constantly challenging mine. That smart mouth that constantly said I was wrong. And then we finally agreed on something—each other. I swear, the first time I tasted you, I could have died. There was nothing sweeter. And then I was a complete *gobaloon*."

"That's putting it mildly," Hannah remarks from the side.

Finn ignores his grandmother. "By the time I realized too much time had passed for me to make a decent apology and everything was *mebs*, I got completely rat arsed."

I cup his cheek. "Finn, all you needed to say was this. We could have talked."

His head crashes down on mine. "But Jenna, it had been donkey's years by that point. And you were you, and I was..."

"You. You've always been you, Finn. Whether you're the uber-sexy Professor Finn O'Roarke making coeds drool or the man who devastated my heart by ensuring his family's happiness—they're both you. And somehow you've made me fall for both of them."

Finn's arms tighten around me as he hauls me up against him. His head descends, and our lips collide. He fits his mouth to mine, and I wrap my arms around his neck. I taste the salty air from the sea mingled with the wine we drank over dinner. But most of all, I taste love—a love I wished for and almost gave up on.

My arms tighten around him as I burrow against him. When our kiss ends, I bury my head against his shoulder, shudders racking my body. Just a few days ago, I was saying I didn't want any more wishes. Now, as I stand there cradled in his arms, I begin whispering all of them in his ear.

I want love. I want a family. I want children. And above all, I want him.

Sometimes the things we hope for should have a chance at coming true.

After every one, Finn promises me he'll do his best to give them to me. And in this place that means so much to him, I believe him.

I believe in us.

Finn slowly turns me around in his arms. "Make a wish, *mo chroí.*" He points at the first star over the horizon.

Out of the corner of my eye, I see Hannah blow a kiss skyward, and tears fill my eyes again. I tip my head back, and he whispers, "She's talking to *seanáthair.* In a moment, we'll help her down so we can prepare for the drive back to Dublin."

I nod against his chest, too moved to speak. As for the wish I just made—that Finn will say yes when I ask him to come back to Connecticut with me after his sister's wedding—I'm certain it's going to come true.

But just to be safe, maybe I'll ask Hannah where she keeps the spare luggage before we leave tonight.

14

JENNA

"You look stunning, Maura." In between the wedding and the reception, I remove her veil and smooth her remarkable hair away from her head using her grandmother's combs—her something old. Her something new is a gorgeous pair of blush-colored heels.

"Her something blue is an excuse of an ensemble her husband should enjoy later," Hannah remarks.

Maura flushes, and Hannah, the scamp, rolls her eyes. "Please. Do you mean to tell me there is nothing going on at the new bed-and-breakfast being built?"

All the women in the room, myself included, try to hide our laughter. Maura is indignant. "*Seanmháthair*, I hope you plan on giving Finn and Rosie this kind of grief on their wedding day."

"Of course not," she replies. Maura looks outraged until Hannah turns her shrewd silver eyes on me. "I plan on speaking with Jenna."

I start to choke on the air I'm breathing. "Hannah, a little warning."

"Why? Are you not the same woman who schemed with me to pack my Finn's clothes for a journey he doesn't yet know he's making?"

"True," I concede. "I planned on asking him after the wedding."

All of the O'Roarkes in the room laugh. Rosie, the one I wanted to choke just a few days earlier, hip bumps me hard enough to almost knock me off my prized Louboutins. "If he doesn't ask you first."

I open my mouth to retort, but then I think about the look in Finn's eyes when he realized the something borrowed in his sister's ears were my treasured Amaryllis earrings. I ponder the question. "Do you think?"

Rosie's answer is "What size are those shoes you're wearing?"

I kick up my heel so the brilliant red sole is displayed. "A 38.5."

Rosie pouts. "Damn me. I was going to bet a walk around in them."

That's when I catch a glimpse of the shiny new diamond on the third finger of Rosie's left hand—something she acquired the night Finn and I saw her at the pub. "How about this, Rosie? If you're right, I'll talk with my stepmother about designing..." I don't even get the words out before she's hugging me so hard, I'm terrified my dress might be riding up.

"Oh, my God. If Finn's not a bleeding idiot, I'll be wearing an Emily Freeman dress, just like Maura." And she bursts into tears.

And that's when I decide, win or lose, I'll make sure Em designs her a dress. After all, one way or another, my wish is coming true. Why shouldn't hers?

With those thoughts, we finish helping Maura and guide her to her impatient husband to be introduced at the reception. I slip into the back of the reception. A handsome man in a tuxedo slips his arm around me. I lean back against him, tipping my head back, waiting for his kiss. "Is she ready, *mo chroí*?"

"She is. You should probably head out to be with the rest of the wedding party," I murmur.

"Not without this." Finn kisses me senseless before he slips out the same door I came in.

And within moments, the music starts.

Hours later, I'm wrapped in Finn's arms, dancing to the Corrs when the sun is setting and the mist of the evening is just starting to

rise, when he asks, "What time do we leave tomorrow?"

I jerk back, startled. "Excuse me?"

He tugs me firmly against his chest. Eyes direct, he repeats his question. "What time do we fly back to America?"

"Finn, are you sure?" My eyes drift over to where Hannah's sitting.

He tips my chin up and says quite clearly, "Do you think I would be so foolish to let love walk away, Jenna?"

I slowly shake my head. "But what about..."

"Rose is going to stay with *seanmháthair* while I am with you in America and Maura is away on her honeymoon. When you travel in Europe, I will come home and visit, but Maura and Will are going to be here with her."

"How does that make you feel?" I whisper.

"Both anxious and exhilarated. I will have the only woman I have ever given my heart to by my side—" His brow hitches.

"You will," I affirm. My head is spinning over his words, particularly the last. *The only woman I have ever given my heart to.* "I love you, Finn, but will it be enough?"

He stops dancing. We're the only two people not moving in a sea of swaying bodies. "Will you kindly repeat that?"

"I love you, Finn, but..."

"There is nothing else but love, Jenna. And I love you. We will carve out a life where wishes coming true aren't an anomaly."

I confess, "My wish is to never live without you."

His smile is the only thing I see before his lips touch mine. "Your wish is my command."

That's when we begin swaying back and forth beneath the single star that appears under the night sky.

I should have known better than to have entered into an argument of any kind with Professor Finn O'Roarke. I can't remember a single time I won one in our tumultuous classroom days. Although it did take him eight days. Finn used them to solidify his position—the one dancing at his sister's wedding being the most persuasive.

Love is always worth wishing for.

But as my head rests against his beating heart, I make a tiny wish. One I hope isn't asking for too much.

I wish for my family to cut him some slack at the family dinner they're preparing upon my return. But even I know that won't take a wish; that will take a miracle.

But that's for tomorrow. Tonight, I just want to dance with Finn's arms wrapped around me. His head lowers, and he whispers his plans for later in my ear. My lips curve. I amend my plans. I lean up and whisper in his ear, "When can we leave to do that?"

"Anytime you want, *mo chroí*. We'll see them all at brunch tomorrow."

"Then let's go."

Finn leads me off the dance floor. We both wave to a few people and make our way up to my room, where our bags are packed for our afternoon departure. I barely give them a passing glance as he leads me directly into the bedroom. As the door closes behind us, my heart explodes with the love shining in his eyes. "I love you, Finn."

"As I love you, Jenna." He pulls me to him and begins to lower the zipper of my dress. Every one of the teeth being let go takes an age but heightens my anticipation. By the time he reaches the end, which rests just below my rear, the strapless dress slips from my body into a pool on the floor, leaving me clad in a tiny scrap of underwear, thigh-highs, and my shoes. I stand before Finn, unashamed of my nudity as he peruses me from head to toe.

And my heart tumbles when he swoops me into his arms, declaring, "It's time to get you out of those wretched shoes."

I wrap my arms around his neck as he crosses the space over to the bed. "I'm fine."

"If it's in my power, nothing will ever hurt you ever again, Jenna." He says this as he slides off my heel and drops it to the side of the bed.

I'd protest the less than careful handling, but he immediately begins rubbing my foot, and it feels so magnificent I squirm on the bed, groaning, "Harder. Right there."

Finn pauses his ministrations. His smile is smug. "You look much like you do when I do this." He leans forward and presses his face between my legs, pushing the ridiculous scrap of lace with his nose before devouring me with his mouth. My back arches, my hips rocking against him as I search for purchase against the smooth Irish linen beneath my hands.

Then I find the one thing I know now I can hold on to—him. Gasping, I thread my fingers into his hair as he snaps one side of my panties to give himself better access before he slips my legs over his shoulders. My one foot, still clad in the spiked heel, must leave marks, but Finn doesn't seem to care as he flicks his tongue back and forth over my clit, tightening the bud before drawing it into his mouth to suck on. Just as my body starts quivering from that alone, he slides two fingers deep inside of me.

And I detonate. "Finn!" His name is a gasp as I listen to his murmured words of love in my ear.

It might be seconds or minutes later, but he slides his now naked body along mine. Lining himself up, he murmurs, "*Mo chroí*," just as his cock begins to enter me.

I wrap my legs around his hips. "And you're mine, Finn."

He pushes forward, slowly. Once our bodies are connected, he leans over to kiss me. He kisses me with one hand on my hip, the other cupping the back of my hair. He continues to kiss me as he begins moving deep inside me, as I lift my hips to take him deeper.

Even after we've both reached the pinnacle of fulfillment, our kiss goes on. It only stops when we fall asleep in each other's arms, not to sleep but to dream more wishes for our tomorrows.

15

FINN

J enna is still shocked when we board the Lockwood company jet to fly back to America. "I can't believe you're a dual citizen!" she exclaims. It shocked her senseless when I departed Ireland with a US passport.

"It's not my fault my parents didn't stay still long enough to have me birthed in the right country."

Jenna socks me in the arm for the crack against America before she takes my hand. "Will you tell me the story?"

"*Mo chroí*, there is nothing of mine you can't have." Squeezing her fingers, I explain to her how my parents—relatively famous archeologists—were being recognized for an unusual find in a Boston museum where they had found a number of scrapers, drills, hammerstones at the DEDIC Site in South Deerfield, Massachusetts. "They returned home briefly, as was their habit, when they found out about the exhibit. My mother was eight and a half months pregnant with me, and though her doctor advised her it wouldn't be wise to travel such a distance, she declared she wasn't missing it for anything in the world."

Jenna mutters under her breath something rude, causing me to laugh as I haul her closer next to me as we fly through the early evening air. "But the true irony, *mo chroí*, is I was troublesome to my parents from the beginning. They had to apply for me to have citizenship in Ireland."

"There's no reciprocity since your parents are citizens?"

"No, there is no unconditional birthright citizenship. Children born in Ireland are Irish citizens if at least one of the parents is an Irish citizen and is settled in either Ireland or has lawfully resided in Ireland for at least three of the four years preceding the child's birth." My mouth quirks to the side. "Can you tell I've done a bit of research about it over the years?"

"Just a bit, Professor. So what did you have to do to apply for citizenship?"

I explain the process to her, and I'm unsurprised when Jenna asks more questions. "But why do you have to leave Ireland on your American passport if you're a dual citizen?" she persists.

"Ah, that's only a requirement when I travel to and from the United States. It is part of your US Immigrations and Nationality Act."

Jenna rubs her temples. "I have so much to learn."

I brush a kiss against the side of her head. "And it doesn't have to happen on a seven-hour plane ride. Now, tell me, where are we staying tonight? At your family's farm?"

She nods. "There are spare rooms in the main building that were converted to an efficiency apartment for me some time back. We'll have until morning to get our bearings before the family begins its descent."

"So, we land at JFK and then..."

Jenna shakes her head. "No, Teterboro. That's where Ryan keeps his plane on standby."

I frown. "What is Teterboro?" In all the time I've flown into the United States, I don't recall having traveled through that airport.

"While technically in New Jersey, it's the most widely used private airport in the United States. It's about ten miles outside of New York, making it very convenient for Ryan, Caleb, Keene—well, any of the family who needs to hop off a quick flight. In fact, when I first came to the farm, Caleb arranged for me and Dad to fly on one of his planes from Nantucket here."

"Caleb? One of his planes?" I probe.

"Right. So, let me explain who's related to whom. There are six Freeman siblings: Phillip, Cassidy, Emily, Alison, Corinna, and Holly. They're married to Jason Ross, Caleb Lockwood, Jake Madison—"

"Your father," I interject.

"Yes, my dad. To round it out, Keene Marshall, Colby Hunt, and Joe Bianco, respectively."

"And Ryan is Caleb's brother?" I question.

Jenna nods. Then she shocks me. "And Keene is Caleb's best friend. Colby knew Corinna, Ali, and Holly in college, but it turns out he's the grandson of a US senator and one of the heirs to Hunt Enterprises."

I choke. "Anyone else I need to be aware of?"

"Just Charlie." Her eyes get a faraway look.

"And who exactly is Charlie?"

She fumbles for a moment, leaving me to wonder if I'm going to be introduced to a former lover. Then I wonder if that might be easier. "Charlie's a retired SEAL. He used to work for Caleb and Keene. Now, well, he's kind of our family protector."

"And what did Caleb and Keene do?"

"Oh, they still do it. They—along with Colby and a host of others —run one of the most successful investigative agencies in the nation." She mentions the company's name before yawning.

"Why don't you curl up, *mo chroí*? We have hours before we land."

"Hmm, maybe for a few minutes. Someone had me up most of the night." Jenna sends me a flirtatious look through the dark fringe of her lashes.

My body immediately reacts to it, but I subdue my baser instincts and encourage her to stretch out so her head is on my thigh. This way I can run my fingers through her hair as I use my other hand to read more about Jenna's family. Instinctively, I have a feeling I'm going to need every bit of knowledge at my disposal.

After Jenna's breathing evens out, I start with her father. Jake

Madison has made quite a name for himself as a songwriter with his cousin-in-law, Brendan Blake. But, as he told an interviewer, "My passion is for teaching. There's something in that moment when music breaks through the heart of a child."

I like the man already.

I spend some time on the Lockwood Industries site, though I studied them well in graduate school. Although I do smile when I see the article about Lynne stepping down to take a position with Bristol Brogan-Houde and her boss's comments lamenting her departure.

Finally, I pull up the website of Hudson Investigations. I read a long time through the press releases, and my mind whirls when I recognize some of the cases this company has been credited with solving. Then I click on the "About" link and read about the owners and department heads: Caleb Lockwood, Keene Marshall, Colby Hunt, Calhoun Sullivan, Samuel Akin, and the recently retired Charles Henderson. After studying their CVs for some time, I close my phone and whisper so Jenna won't waken, "I'm not making it out of this family dinner alive, am I? So, know I love you with every breath in my body, *mo chroí*."

Jenna sleeps on, but I don't close my eyes at all during the flight, figuring I'll sleep when I'm dead, which may be sooner than I anticipated.

Waking with my arms wrapped around Jenna is the most remarkable feeling in the world. We start to rouse from our morning haze when someone begins blaring Sia on the stereo just as fists pound out the beat on our door. A male voice yells, "Jenna, get yours and the professor's asses out of bed. Corinna's cooking!"

She moans before reaching blindly for something. "Go away, Uncle Phil. We didn't get to bed until late."

"Just because you decided to jump the man...ow! Damnit, Em. That hurt!"

"I'll do more than that if you don't get away from Jenna's door, you ass."

Without having spoken a word directly to her, I immediately decide I love Jenna's stepmother. But Jenna's now in an upright position, scrambling for something to throw on. "Em? Wait. Don't leave. I want you to meet Finn!" Immediately after she says that, my pants smack me in the head.

That's when Phil says, "See? We'll get to meet him before the others."

"She said 'Em.' Is your name Em?" Em asks with exasperation in her voice.

"*Mo chroí*, is it always like this?" I ask carefully as she's running across the bed naked in an effort to locate my shirt. Not for me so I can meet her family for the first time fully dressed, I note with some amusement as I slide into my slacks and Jenna shrugs it on over her bare shoulders, but just to cover herself up so she can fling her door open and leap into Em's arms. The two women embrace like it's been years since they've seen one another, not like they didn't just talk via FaceTime a few days ago.

"Oh, it's so good to hold you," Em breathes into her stepdaughter's hair before pulling back a bit. What she sees there must satisfy her because she loops an arm around Jenna's waist and holds out her hand. "Professor O'Roarke, I'm Emily Freeman-Madison."

"It's Finn, please, Ms. Freeman-Madison." I hold out my own hand as well. "And perhaps this conversation will be less awkward if I start it out by telling you I'm irrevocably in love with Jenna."

A bright glint appears behind Em's eyes. Her smile goes wonky. "I figured you must be or you wouldn't be here, Finn. Our family is a very close one."

Phil shoves his way forward, hand extended. "Phillip Freeman-Ross."

"Finn O'Roarke." I take his hand and accept the threat in his eyes easily because it's born out of something I understand—love of Jenna.

"As the eldest in the family, it's my duty to inform you that if you—"

"For all that's holy, Phil," Em snaps. "Aren't there going to be enough threats of dismemberment over breakfast?"

Jenna slides away from her stepmother and steps next to me. My arm slides around her shoulder, hers around my waist. She carefully asks, "What are you talking about, Em?"

"Normally you know I'd be murdering Phil for waking you up, but honey, it's not going to be a family dinner. Everyone's on their way."

"Right now? They couldn't even give me a morning to settle back in?" Jenna shrieks.

"Apparently Ryan talked to Caleb, who did some digging on Finn. They're not waiting. And if it wasn't for the kids, you know your father would be right here, right now." Em shoots me a pained look.

Jenna yells, "I love you both, but get out. I haven't begun to unpack."

Phil remarks, "I noticed. That's unusual for you. Were you too busy..."

That's when I drop my arm from Jenna and step forward in front of the older man. "I'd hate to get off on a bad note with Jenna's family by dropping her uncle for disrespecting her life, her choices, instead of honoring them."

Precious moments tick by before Em declares, "I'm Team Finn."

Phil surprisingly agrees. "So am I. We'll leave you both to get ready. If you hurry, you can meet the rest of the sisters before the others arrive."

Both Em and Phil leave Jenna's suite with a hasty goodbye. The moment they do, Jenna throws herself at me. I stumble back as I catch her in my arms. She begins peppering my face with kisses. "Darling, we definitely do not have time for this," I warn her as she rubs herself up against me, despite the rising of my cock behind the zipper of my trousers.

"We'll shower together. Two birds, one stone."

And considering my cock feels just like that, I turn and carry her directly into the en suite. It was fast and hard, but if I'm going to die in a few minutes, I'll have her lips on my skin as the last thing I feel.

Jenna forsakes her morning routine, throwing on jeans and a T-shirt, feet bare. I dress much the same, slipping into a pair of jeans and a short-sleeve Henley, but slide my feet into leather driving shoes. With barely two minutes to spare, we're flinging open the door and find a man waiting outside who is Jenna's spitting image.

Her father.

She leaps into his arms, her welcome completely assured. "Dad! I have so much to tell you."

It's disconcerting to find the eyes of the woman you love in another's face. Especially when they're stinging you with disapproval. But none of that is in his voice when he kisses her head, murmuring, "So I heard. Let's get some food so I don't kill your boyfriend."

"Dad, let me introduce you to—"

"Jen, I'm really not kidding about the killing part. At least let me get a cinnamon roll in me before you start talking."

And then, Jenna digs in her dainty heels. "No."

"Excuse me?" Jake Madison's mouth thins.

I step forward to support Jenna just as she reaches for me. "I won't let you nor any member of the family make me feel like anything I did, anything I felt, was shameful."

His dark brown eyes skewer me. "He's thirteen years your senior, Jenna."

"So what?" she snaps. "Do you want me to go through the age gaps of some of the family members? Maybe Holly and Joe would like it pointed out she's older than he is."

"He was your professor," her father growls.

"Not at the time. In fact, I'd just turned in my last assignment, which for the record, he graded me even harder on."

It's then I admit, "Which I never actually graded." Both father and daughter gape at me. "I was called home for a death in my family, so one of my colleagues graded your final assignment, Jenna. I kept meaning to tell you that."

Her mouth opens and closes like a fish before she manages, "You let me berate you for ruining my GPA."

"Well, I figured it was partially true."

"How do you figure that?" she demands, hands planted akimbo.

"If you'd actually been paying attention in class instead of persistently arguing with me, you might not have botched that pop quiz on Dale Carnegie. Then you wouldn't have been so reliant on a perfect score to get your summa cum laude," I return easily.

Jenna makes an odd squeaking sound before she throws up her hands and storms off, leaving her father and me alone in the hall outside of her room. He gives me a head-to-toe perusal before stating, "No one will ever be good enough for her."

"I know. But every day I'll do my damnedest to try. That's all anyone can do, really. And knowing Jenna, when that's not enough, she'll kick my arse."

He barks out a laugh. "You really love her?"

When I face him, there's anguish running through every inch of his body. "With everything I am."

He looks away before nodding. When he turns back, he holds out a hand. "You're going to need an ally down there."

"Your wife implied as much. She and Phil..."

That's when Jake Madison roars with laughter. "Good God, don't align yourself with Phil. Keene will eat you alive, enjoy it, and the others will be laughing too hard to be much help. Now if you want to survive, take it from someone who confronted them head-on and walked out alive."

I cock my head to the side. "How did you do that, Mr. Madison?"

"Make it Jake, Finn. Once my daughter starts speaking to you again, I'll tell you that story. Say, how is it you're an American citizen?"

By this point, we've made our way down the stairs. Waiting for us are four of the most intense men I've ever seen. My legs begin to shake so hard at the uncompromising expressions on their faces. These men have encouraged Jenna to fly while helping protect her.

But what I won't do is be daunted by them. "I won't apologize for loving her, then or now. She saw me, inside me, and challenged me to be a better man. I gave her years to fly—to find someone better than me—but we're linked through the trinity: mind, body, and soul. And I will tolerate anything you have to throw at me but will do my damnedest to prevent an ounce of pain from reaching her."

Keene Marshall's and Caleb Lockwood's faces relax moderately. "Since we're all big believers in fate, I can't help but agree with what the good professor said," Caleb says quietly across to Keene.

Keene nods. "Which means we can't kill him? Can we still torture him?"

Frantically, I struggle to find an escape. That's when the third man, Colby Hunt, enters the conversation. He's munching on the aforementioned cinnamon rolls. "Jenna will be seriously pissed. Plus, I don't want to deal with my wife over it. And neither do any of you seeing as she'll never bake for you again."

Keene grunts. Caleb claps my shoulder, murmuring, "She's the first of the next generation to fall, Finn?" I nod. "Finn, she's our niece in every way that matters. We love her too."

"I can appreciate that. And I also know she's missed all of you terribly."

Keene holds out a hand for me to shake. I take it and find myself being interrogated without a word. "So, does Jenna know you've already been looking at property in the area? Or is that supposed to be a surprise?"

I start to choke. Jake wails on my back cheerfully. "A surprise. I'm still waiting to hear back from the school about the job I applied for."

We begin to make our way into the kitchen. "Another university?" Jake asks conversationally.

Just then, Jenna's eyes meet mine across the expanse of the kitchen. Her look of relief is mingled with an intense love so fierce, I'm distracted when I say, "No, a local high school. It turns out they're looking for an economics professor. This way, I'd have more stable hours when we decide to start having a family, and Jenna wouldn't have to curtail her work at Amaryllis Events."

All of the men murmur their approval, except her father. His voice is horrified when he exclaims, "Not Ridgefield High School."

I'm startled and pleased to say, "Yes. That's the school. Lovely place from the pictures I've been privy to."

"You absolutely cannot teach there," he states adamantly.

"Why not?" There's raucous laughter around me. "Is there something I'm missing?"

"Yes. I'm the head of the music department there. And the idea of having my daughter's boyfriend teach at the same school is..." His voice trails off as he turns introspective.

"What?" I ask impatiently. And I don't correct him that it will be son-in-law soon enough.

Jake laughs. "Actually, never mind. It's perfect."

I anxiously ask, "Do you think Jenna will be upset?"

That's when I hear her voice. "Upset? You'd give up living in Ireland for me?" I whirl around and face her to find tears streaking down her face.

"*Mo chroí*, I'd give up anything for you. Don't you know that by now?"

Jenna reaches up and pulls my face close enough to lay her lips on mine before she whispers, "I forgive you for that A minus now."

"I'm so grateful."

Jenna grins up at me. "You should be."

She has no idea. Even as I'm giving thanks, she rises up on the ball of her feet to whisper, "What are you wishing for, Finn?"

"Anything, as long as it's with you," I tell her honestly.

As I lower my head to kiss her, I hear Jake mutter, "He makes her happy, and that's all I ever wanted for her from the moment she was born. Damnit."

EPILOGUE

JENNA-PRESENT DAY

Tenderly, I drag my finger down the cheek of our newborn daughter. It's the first time we've been alone since coming home from the hospital five days ago. Understandable, really, with Finn's and my families descending to meet her. But now the excitement's died down, I have an important story to share.

"Hannah, there's going to be many things we teach you over the years. But the most important thing to remember is—" I'm interrupted by the door opening.

Finn strolls in bearing a tray filled with goodies, including a blue box tied with a white bow. "Why do you have a guilty look on your face, Jenna?" he demands.

"I don't know what you mean."

Plunking the tray down on a nearby table, Finn stalks over to the bed. "I thought we decided to tell her together." The same pique that used to appear on his face when I'd disagree with him in class crosses his face.

It turned me on then; it still does today.

Fortunately, now I can do what I want to make it disappear. Pulling him close, I kiss him with all the love in my heart. "I only just started," I whisper against his lips.

Crawling onto the bed next to me, he wraps both of us up in his strong arms. "I foolishly sent your mother away to make a wish upon the stars," he says hollowly.

Smiling tenderly, I murmur, "I hadn't got there yet."

"Oh." He nuzzles the hair away from my neck before pressing his lips there. "How far along were you?"

As I'm wrapped in his arms, as Finn's teeth rake along my neck, I realize Hannah doesn't need to know about the years we lost. Nor do I need to share the passion that exploded between us when we reunited. All she needs to know is, "Once upon a time, there was a princess who was free to wish. And she loved making wishes more than anything."

Wetness from Finn's eyes drips down onto my bare shoulder as I tell an abbreviated version of our story to our daughter.

One day, she might need to know it all as she fights for her own happily ever after. But not today.

WHERE TO GET HELP

People sometimes have difficulty with "age of consent" or "power of authority" tropes in romance because of emotional scarring. And I certainly hope Jenna and Finn's story didn't cause those emotions for you.

I needed to write their story because I've had a front-row seat to a beautiful love story where as many as twenty years separated the husband and wife. And they were together until death separated one from the other.

Unfortunately, I've also had to bear witness to the opposite end of the spectrum where power was abused in a grossly horrific manner—something that should happen to no woman.

Nor to any man.

As a human, you should be comfortable in your surroundings. If you are not, and if you need help, report it to the authorities at your location. And remember, if you need to talk and you're not certain if anyone will listen, you can always get help 24 hours a day, seven days a week at the Rape, Abuse & Incest National Network (RAINN - https://www.rainn.org/).

Life happens at both ends of the spectrum—the good and the

bad. Just remember, amid reality, there is hope and love waiting for all of us.

ACKNOWLEDGMENTS

To my husband, I was already granted my most important wish—you. I love you more with every word I type.

To my son. My little leprechaun. Oh, God. You're as tall as me! How can this be? I love you, baby.

To my mother, who brought me enough coffee and biscuits to survive writing another book amidst chaos.

To my Jen. You know for all the reasons why. Don't make me cry when I'm writing this. I love you!

To my Meows, for showing me there's magic everywhere. I love you all. Ireland 2022?

To Sandra Depukat, from One Love Editing, I'm counting down the days until I can hug you again. Even if I have to take a red-eye to get there.

To Holly Malgieri, from Comma Sutra Editorial, for making the first "dream" come true.

To Amy Queue, QDesigns. How perfect this was set in Ireland, my fey, friend! Thank you for the magic with this cover!

To Gel, at Tempting Illustrations, always beautiful. Thank you!

To the fantastic team at Foreword PR, there's not enough ways to thank you! You're all my stars!

Linda Russell, I'm not certain how I get through this without you by my side. I love you.

To my Musketeers. Close your eyes and make a wish. We're almost there. #unbreakable

To Susan Henn, Amy Rhodes, and Dawn Hurst. Each of you brings something special to every book. Keep sparkling.

For the amazing individuals who are a part of Tracey's Tribe, thank you for starting the first Freeman hangout!

And to the readers and bloggers who take the time to enjoy my books, you are the real stars. Thank you.

Now, who should I write next?

ABOUT THE AUTHOR

Tracey Jerald knew she was meant to be a writer when she would re-write the ending of books in her head on her bike when she was a young girl growing up in southern Connecticut. It wasn't long before she was typing alternate endings and extended epilogues "just for fun".

After college in Florida, where she obtained a degree in Criminal Justice swearing she saw things she'll never quite believe and never quite forget, Tracey traded the world of law and order for IT. Her work for a world-wide internet startup transferred her to Northern Virginia where she met her husband in what many call their own happily ever after. They have one son.

When she's not busy with her family or writing, Tracey can be found in her home in north Florida drinking coffee, reading, training for a runDisney event, or feeding her addiction to HGTV.

To follow Tracey, go to her website at https://www.traceyjerald.com.

Made in the USA
Las Vegas, NV
11 October 2021